CURSE THE DAY

A SPELLBOUND PARANORMAL COZY MYSTERY,
BOOK 1

ANNABEL CHASE

RED PALM PRESS LLC

Curse the Day

A Spellbound Paranormal Cozy Mystery, Book 1

By Annabel Chase

Sign up for my newsletter here http://eepurl.com/ctYNzf and or like me on Facebook so you can find out about new releases.

Cover Design by Alchemy

❀ Created with Vellum

To the Tiki Bar Mastermind Group – you're the best!
Thanks for all the love and support.

CHAPTER 1

FOUR POINT seven miles to go.

I peered through the windshield at the towering evergreens and intimidating rock formations. How could anyone possibly live around here? There were no houses in sight. The only signs of life were road-kill so...okay, no signs of life then. Even the radio station had given up. At least my phone was—

Uh oh.

The screen was still telling me to turn right in four point seven miles. Sayonara signal.

"This day gets more perfect by the minute." It started off on the wrong foot when the battery in my alarm clock chose today to die after I'd struggled through another night of insomnia. Then I couldn't find a matching pair of trouser socks thanks to the hungry sock monster that apparently lived in the tumble dryer in the basement of my apartment building. So now I was the proud wearer of one navy blue sock and one black sock. Close enough that the client wouldn't notice...probably because she'd be too busy berating me for my tardiness. Without a phone signal, I couldn't even call to let her know. I hoped she was the forgiving type. I didn't have much information beyond her name, phone number, and address since this was to be our first time meeting.

I watched intently for signs of a right turn. Any sign. Eventually, I came upon a dirt road.

"I guess this is it." It was only wide enough for one car. "Let's hope I don't run into a bus." Literally.

The road became increasingly bumpy and I worried for my car. It was a green Volvo—okay, more specifically it was a 1988 beat-up green Volvo that I inherited from my grandmother after she died. My own parents died when I was young, so I was raised by my father's parents. Grandpa died first and then Gran died three years ago, leaving me all alone.

"This can't possibly be the right road," I said.

Although the setting was beautiful, there was no sign of civilization. A shimmering lake came into view on my right. With looming boulders and majestic trees, it was incredibly scenic.

Except for the guy standing on the edge of the cliff, ready to jump.

Wait. What?

"Don't do it," I shouted, not that he could hear me. Under the circumstances, was it wrong to notice how incredibly gorgeous he was?

I began beeping the horn. He looked at me in surprise. I guess he counted on complete solitude for his suicide mission. There was no sign of another vehicle. I wondered how he managed to get here. Or up there. That clifftop was high enough to make my palms sweaty.

He turned his attention back to the lake and stood erect, poised for action. I couldn't tear my gaze away. I set the parking brake, released the clutch, and threw open my car door. I raced toward the water's edge. Waving my arms frantically, I hoped to catch his attention. To stop him from making a huge mistake.

"Don't jump," I shrieked, running the length of the dock that led to the middle of the lake.

His white wings spread out behind him.

His wings?

He swooped down from the cliff and headed straight for me. Holy Flying Hot Guy. Was he angry that I interrupted his plans? Was he going to hurt me?

I froze in place. It was only then that I heard the sound of my car's motor coming closer.

I whipped around to see my Volvo behind me, crushing the wooden planks as it hurtled toward me. Damn parking brake! There was only one way to avoid being crushed. I closed my eyes, held my nose, and jumped off the edge of the dock. Either way, I was about to die.

I kept waiting to hit the water, but it didn't happen. I heard a loud splash and opened my eyes in time to see my beloved Volvo nosedive into the lake.

It was then I noticed the strong arms around me and the small fact that I was airborne.

I was airborne.

The winged man whisked me safely to the cliff's edge, where he'd stood only moments ago, just in time to watch the lake swallow the back end of my car.

I stared into the winged man's beautiful face, uncertain what to say.

"Are you my guardian angel?" I asked. *And, if so, where in the hell have you been for the past twenty-five years?* Wait, could I say 'hell' to my guardian angel?

"Absolutely not," he said gruffly. He released me

and my legs turned to jelly, forcing him to grab me again so I didn't fall off the cliff.

"Well, I guess I'm yours," I said, still shaking.

He looked at me askance. "How do you figure that?"

"Um, hello?" I pointed to the water far below. "You were about to end it all."

He displayed his wings again. "If I was going to end it all, I don't think jumping from a great height would be the logical choice for me."

When I reached out to touch the feathers, he smacked my hand away.

"They can't be real," I murmured. "This has to be an elaborate joke."

"You're telling me," he said. "This is my safe place. No one ever bothers me here."

"Shouldn't your safe place be a little higher up?" I queried, pointing skyward.

"A story for another time," he said. "How can you even see me?"

"The cliff isn't *that* high," I replied.

He eyed me suspiciously. "Did you know you had the Sight?"

"Well, I've been using my eyes since birth so…yes?"

He groaned. "Not sight. The Sight. The Third

Eye. Piercing the Veil." He poked the spot on my forehead between my eyes. "It's a particular human gift that allows them to see through supernatural glamours and such. Ring any bells?"

I shook my head. Being this close to him on a clifftop was making me nervous.

"If you just drop me back on the shore of the lake, I'll see what I can do about my car." Never mind that my phone and handbag were in the bottom of the lake, along with my car.

He pressed his lips together. "Can't do it, I'm afraid."

"Sure you can. Just spread those wings of yours and fly me over."

His expression clouded over. "No, I can't. The dock's been destroyed thanks to your monster on wheels and the boundary is in the middle of the lake. If you'd been any closer to the shore, I wouldn't have been able to help you." He tapped his finger on his chin. "I suppose I could drop you gently into the middle of the lake and you can swim back to shore." He considered me for a moment. "You held your nose when you jumped."

"Did not."

"Sure you did."

"Okay, fine. I'm not the best swimmer." Truth be told, I couldn't swim at all and was deathly afraid of the water. Not like I had many occasions to learn when I was growing up. My grandparents didn't take trips to the beach and we didn't know anyone with a pool.

"That presents a problem then."

"Why does it matter about the dock? Just drop me on the other side of the lake." And I'll forget this whole thing ever happened with copious amounts of alcohol.

"I told you. The boundary's in the middle of the lake."

My brow creased. "The boundary for where?"

"For the town where I live. Spellbound."

"Your town is called Spellbound?" I'd never heard of a town with that name, certainly not in Pennsylvania.

"Don't give me that look. I didn't name it." He held up a finger. "I know. I'll take you to the forest border. It's not ideal because you'll need to walk further, but it's better than nothing."

I tried to wrap my head around what he was saying. "The forest border?"

"You know what a forest is, don't you?" he said, and then seemed distracted by something on the ground in front of me. "Do you know your socks don't match?"

I glanced down at my feet. How could he possibly tell? My shoes covered most of the mismatched material. "It's the style."

"Not in any century I've ever lived in."

I started to laugh. "This has to be the most elaborate hoax anyone has ever played on me." I patted him on the shoulder, searching for the invisible wires. "Good job, Michael. Seriously, you're a pro."

"Michael?"

"Aren't all angels named Michael?"

He stuck out his hand. "Daniel. Nice to meet you."

"Emma," I said, and shook his hand. "Emma Hart."

"Hold on tight, Emma, and I'll take you over to the forest border."

I folded my arms. "Not until you tell me how you're able to fly, Peter Pan." I wasn't a fan of heights.

"I would think telling you I'm an angel would be explanation enough."

"You're talking to someone who would rather take a three-day train journey than ride inside a flying metal death tube."

His mouth quirked. “Do you mean an airplane?”

“Ever run into one of those?” I pointed skyward.

“I see them fly overhead all the time,” he replied. “They appear perfectly safe.” He motioned for me to move closer. “Come on. The sooner I get you to the forest border, the sooner you can get help with your car.”

I looped my arms around his neck and squeezed my eyes shut. The wind swelled around us and I felt my stomach drop when we were airborne again. My heart thundered in my chest. I couldn’t bear to look. I was still fairly convinced I was dreaming. Maybe when I opened my eyes, I’d be back in bed with a working alarm clock, about to hit the snooze button for the sixth time.

“We’re here,” Daniel said.

I popped one eye open and looked around. We did, indeed, seem to be in the forest.

“Where’s the town?” I asked.

He jerked a thumb behind him. “I took you as close to the border as I can get.”

“How far do you suppose I’ll need to walk?” I asked. I didn’t love the idea of traipsing through the forest alone. This whole area was desolate and I had no way of contacting anyone.

"No clue." He patted me on the back. "Good luck, though."

I took a hesitant step forward and turned back. "Are you really an angel?"

He nodded grimly. "Trust me. It's not all it's cracked up to be."

"Well, thanks for saving me when I thought I was saving you. I appreciate it."

A genuine smile formed on his lips and that simple gesture changed his entire face. He was already incredibly handsome, but the smile transformed him into someone swoonworthy. "And thanks for wanting to save me. It was...unexpected."

I continued to stand there staring at him, lost in those aquamarine eyes. They were the color of every exotic sea I'd never visited. I was so mesmerized that I couldn't even name one. Wait, the Mediterranean. There.

Daniel gestured to the gap between two white birch trees. "There you go. Your exit strategy awaits."

I nodded mutely and forced myself toward the gap. No one would believe my story. My internet article would end up with a thousand hateful comments about damning my soul to hell, along with a couple of Russian women wanting to date me.

I gave one last glance over my shoulder before I

stepped between the trees. Daniel was watching me, a wistful expression etched in his handsome features.

I took one last step and—

"Ouch!" I stopped and rubbed my nose. It felt like I'd walked bang into a tree except there wasn't anything in front of me.

I stepped forward again, only to hit an invisible wall. I turned and looked helplessly at Daniel.

"Is there some kind of invisible force field?"

His brow furrowed. "You can't get out?"

I pressed my hands against the invisible barrier. It was like putting my palms against cold steel. "Apparently not."

"Uh oh," Daniel said.

I whirled around. "Uh oh? What does that mean?"

He gave me a sheepish look. "I think you'd better come with me."

CHAPTER 2

He flew me to the center of town. Spellbound was unlike any place I'd ever seen. Imagine every picture postcard European village meshed with a magic-filled theme park and you might be close.

"Where are we going?" I asked. "Why can't I leave?"

"I'm not sure," he replied. "Just try to hold off on the questions until I can get some answers."

We stopped outside a brick building. The sign read 'Registrar's Office' in fancy script. The only time I'd ever been in a registrar's office was for college and law school.

"Why are we going in here?" I asked.

"Patience is a virtue," he said, and opened the door. The thin man behind the desk gave us a curious look as we stepped inside.

"Good morning, Daniel," the man said, somewhat surprised. His ears were pointier than Captain Spock's. I resisted the urge to stare and focused on the painting behind him instead. It depicted five werewolves smoking cigars and playing poker.

Werewolves?

"Stan," Daniel greeted him gruffly. "We have a situation."

"I'm a situation?" I asked.

"You don't happen to have an Emma Hart on your list, do you?" Daniel asked.

Stan shook his head. "Can't say that I do. Is this the young lady in question?"

"I am," I said, still confused. "Why can't I cross the border and get back to my car?" Or what was left of my car, once I had it fished out of the lake.

Stan's thin brow lifted. "I see." He scrutinized me. "You're human, you say?"

"I do say." Although not very often. I didn't usually need to specify my species.

Stan and Daniel exchanged meaningful glances.

"How did she get here?" Stan asked.

Daniel relayed the story, gallantly leaving out the part where I held my nose. "So what do we do?" he asked.

"This is rather unprecedented," Stan said, swallowing hard. "I suppose we ought to call on Mayor Knightsbridge."

Daniel groaned. "I'm not dealing with that battle axe. She'll spend ninety percent of the conversation blaming me."

Stan looked down his nose at the angel. "It was her *daughter,* Daniel. Can you blame the woman?"

Daniel muttered something unintelligible under his breath. He was proving a bit testy for an angel.

"If it's a problem, I'll go see the mayor on my own," I said. I wasn't intimidated by authority. I'd lost count of the number of times I stood and argued before a judge I didn't respect.

"Oh no," Stan protested. "I wouldn't advise that. Felicity Knightsbridge is not to be trifled with."

"She's difficult at the best of times," Daniel added.

"I don't want to trifle with her," I said, whatever that meant. "I just want to get my car out of the lake and get home. I need to call my client. She's going to wonder what happened to me."

"Your client?" Stan queried.

"I'm a lawyer," I said. "I was on my way to see a client when I got lost and passed by the lake." I shot Daniel a disapproving look. "You know the rest."

"A lawyer, eh?" Stan said.

"No lawyer jokes," I said, waving my hands.

"Especially none that involve lawyers at the bottom of a lake." It hit too close to home at the moment.

"No, no," Stan said. "I wasn't going to make a joke. I was simply..."

Daniel cut him off. "I don't think Emma needs to hear about the dark underbelly of Spellbound."

Stan shrugged. "She might, if she's going to live here."

"Live here?" I blurted. "I have no intention of staying here another hour."

"Come on," Daniel said, and edged toward the door. "Let's go see Mayor Knightsbridge."

As we walked down the cobblestone, I noticed the sign for the town council building. "Isn't that where we're going?"

Daniel laughed. "No, the mayor prefers to work out of her home. It's called the Mayor's Mansion."

The Mayor's Mansion was not an exaggeration.

The stone building loomed at the top of a hill. The style was more gothic than administrative.

"Why does she work from here?" I asked.

"Because she can," Daniel replied flatly.

We trudged up the massive stone steps and were greeted by two guards that reminded me of the

Beefeaters in front of Buckingham Palace. Their hats were black and adorned with green plumes.

"What's with all the pomp and circumstance?" I asked.

"That's fairies for you," he grumbled.

Fairies. Wow. I needed a drink.

The foyer was even grander than the outside. Large portraits and tapestries covered every available inch of wall space. It was like stepping into a functional medieval castle.

A young woman fluttered toward us. I say fluttered because she didn't walk. She sported small pink wings that lifted her off the floor intermittently.

"Mr. Starr," she said, showing off her dimpled cheeks.

"Hello, Lucy," he said. "Is the mayor available? It's rather an emergency."

Lucy looked me up and down, her expression revealing nothing. "She's incredibly busy with the murder and all—everyone's very upset—but I'll see what I can do."

"The murder?" I asked, after Lucy retreated to the mayor's office.

"Nothing to worry about. Spellbound has a crime rate like anywhere else."

Lucy whizzed back in a hurry. "She can squeeze you in now."

"Most appreciated," Daniel said, tucking his wings away. They were like bifold doors on his back but prettier.

We followed Lucy down a long corridor to a room at the back of the mansion. The mayor's office was enormous. Three out of four walls were lined with books. The fourth wall was made entirely of glass and overlooked the backyard. An oversized desk sat in front of the glass wall.

Mayor Knightsbridge glanced up when we entered and quickly closed the file she was reviewing.

"Thank you, Lucy," she said, her lips forming a thin line. She did not seem happy to see Daniel.

"Mayor Knightsbridge, thank you for seeing us on short notice."

The mayor looked from Daniel to me. "Us, is it? How interesting. Seems like only yesterday you were courting my daughter."

"It was decades ago," he mumbled.

I waved my hands. "There's no us, Madam Mayor. He just means..."

The mayor snapped her fingers and my mouth

clamped shut. I tried to speak but couldn't seem to force my lips apart.

"I did not address you," Mayor Knightsbridge said haughtily. She returned her focus to Daniel. "Who is this and why is she in Spellbound?"

He told the story again. "She thinks she's a human," he added. "But she can't be, right? I mean, she'd be able to leave."

"Indeed." She came out from behind her desk and stood directly in front of me. She was about four inches shorter than me with blond hair swept up in a French twist. Her blue wings were larger than Lucy's but not as large as Daniel's.

"What is your name?" She snapped her fingers again and my lips broke apart.

"Emma Hart," I said. "I'm a lawyer from Lemon Grove, Pennsylvania."

"Who are your parents?" she asked. Even at close range, her skin was flawless. No fair.

"I was raised by my father's parents," I said. "Byron and Nancy Hart. My mom died when I was three and my father died when I was seven."

"And your mother's parents?" she asked, peering at me.

"I don't know. I never met them. They died before I was born." Revealing such personal information to strangers made me feel extremely vulnerable, not to mention uncomfortable. It wasn't a subject I discussed with anyone, even boyfriends. Not that there'd been any of those in quite some time.

"What was your mother's name?" the mayor asked.

"Geri White."

"Short for Gertrude?"

My eyes widened. "How did you know?" People generally assumed her full name was Geraldine.

Mayor Knightsbridge ignored my question. "Take her to the coven for confirmation."

Daniel cleared his throat. "The coven? Really?"

The mayor nodded crisply. "I believe so."

I opened my mouth but no sound came out. This time it wasn't due to the mayor's magical snaps.

"Excuse me, Mayor?"

"Yes, Mr. Starr?"

"Is there no one in your office who can escort her?" Daniel asked. "I have a busy day."

"Yes, a busy day of moping, I'm sure," the mayor said. "I'm afraid there's no one available. My office is preoccupied with Gareth's murder at the moment. You created this mess. Miss Hart is your responsibility until the council convenes to discuss the matter."

I snuck a peek at Daniel out of the corner of my eye. He didn't seem happy about being appointed my guardian. Not that I blamed him. I wasn't happy about having a guardian appointed for me.

"What time will the council meet?" he asked.

She gave him a sharp look and he turned on his heel and marched me out of the office.

"Are we really going to a coven?" I asked, hurrying to catch up as he left the mansion in an angelic fury.

"Not a coven," he said. "*The* coven."

Well, that explained it then.

We flew this time.

Daniel carried me in his arms like I'd watched Superman carry Lois Lane countless times, except Daniel didn't wear a unitard. Small favors.

This time I forced my eyes to stay open so I could watch the town pass beneath our feet. No easy feat for someone with my anxiety issues. It was, for lack of a better word, magical. I saw the church spire on a distant hill and the clock tower in the town square. The town was bustling with people, or creatures that looked remarkably like people, and the buildings seemed to stretch beyond the horizon.

I still felt the need to pinch myself. Today I'd met an angel, two fairies, and what I was fairly certain was an elf. And now I was about to meet a coven of witches. It was an amazingly lucid dream and I was sure I'd awaken at any moment. Never again would I eat the entire bag of Doritos before bed.

We landed in front of an apothecary shop.

"The coven is here?" I queried.

"The members we want to see are."

It wasn't what I expected, not that I had any clue what a real coven was like.

We entered the shop and Daniel greeted two teen girls behind the counter. They both batted their eyelashes at him like they'd never seen a member of the opposite sex before.

"They're witches?" I whispered.

"Yes, two of the younger ones. They were born here." Something in his tone suggested that being born here was different from moving here.

"I need to see Ginger," he said.

"This way, Mr. Starr," the smaller of the two girls said. She brought us behind the counter and pushed aside a set of heavy velvet drapes.

"Someone will meet you on the other side," the

girl said, giggling as she scurried back to the counter.

Daniel pulled on a thick rope that hung beside the large wooden door. The door opened by itself and I followed Daniel inside. There was no one in the foyer to greet us.

"Where do we go?" I asked.

A voice interrupted us before he could reply.

"Well, well. What could possibly be important enough to bring Mr. Starr into the belly of the beast?" A woman stepped out of the shadows. Her red hair was pulled back tightly in a high ponytail and she had a sprinkle of freckles across the bridge of her nose. Instead of the long, black cloak I expected her to wear, she sported yoga pants and a half top with the words 'Girl Power' spelled out in glitter.

"Good morning, Ginger," he said tersely.

She narrowed her eyes at me. "I don't recognize this one. Where'd you pick her up?"

"Mayor Knightsbridge thinks she's one of yours. She asked me to bring her to you."

I choked back laughter. "One of theirs? Are you serious? I'm not a witch."

Ginger stared at me with renewed interest. "A new witch in Spellbound? How?"

Daniel grimaced. "She accidentally crossed the border and then couldn't get out."

Ginger's smile broadened. "Fascinating." She circled me, drinking in every detail of my appearance.

"I'm twenty-five years old," I said. "I'm pretty sure I'd know by now if I was a witch."

"Not necessarily," Ginger said. "What's your name, honey?"

"Emma Hart."

She looped her arm through mine. "Emma Hart, you are going to have the best time here."

I looked to Daniel for help, but he only shrugged.

"Is there some sort of test that I take?" I asked. "I mean, what happens if I'm not a witch. What else could I be?"

Ginger ticked off the options on her fingers. "Succubus, fairy, elf, siren, dwarf, Valkyrie, banshee." She waved a dismissive hand. "Oh, a bunch more, but it doesn't matter. I'd bet a cauldron of newt eyes that you're one of us."

"What makes you say that?" I asked.

"Because Daniel found you," she said, and winked at him. "He's always been drawn to witches. Haven't you, Halo Boy?"

"Never mind my life story, Ginger," he said.

Ginger placed a proprietary arm around my shoulder. "We'll take it from here, honey. Thanks for dropping her off."

"But my car is still at the bottom of the lake," I said. "And my phone and my purse...I need to call my client."

Ginger gave me a sad smile. "We might be able to salvage your car, but I'm afraid the phone call is impossible."

Damn.

"We need to decide how to handle her," Ginger continued. "Her arrival is unprecedented."

"The council will decide," Daniel said. "The mayor has already called an emergency meeting."

"Good to know," Ginger replied.

"You'll be fine, Emma," Daniel said, with a trace of uncertainty.

"Thank you for your help today," I said. Sort of.

"I'm sorry," he blurted. "I didn't know this would happen."

"It's okay," I told him. "You said the boundary is in the middle of the lake and I was already there. You just saved me from getting squashed by Sigmund."

"Sigmund?" he queried.

"My car. That's his name."

"She named her car," Ginger said with a cackle.

"Oh, she's definitely one of us. Come along, honey. I'll introduce you to some of the girls."

Ginger brought me to a room upstairs where a dozen women were partway through an exercise class. If they thought I could lift my leg as high as what I'd just witnessed, they'd be sadly mistaken. I couldn't possibly be one of them.

"Everyone, we have a special guest. This is Emma Hart," Ginger said.

The music stopped abruptly and the entire room turned to stare at me. It was like junior high school all over again.

"Hello," I said weakly.

"Her socks don't match," I heard someone whisper.

Yep. Just like junior high.

A tall, redheaded woman in the center of the room strode toward me. She looked like Ginger, only slightly older but with the same killer body. She lifted her shirt to wipe a few droplets of sweat from her brow and I saw a flash of perfect abs. So much for warts and green skin.

"How is this possible?" the woman asked.

"Long story," Ginger said.

"How did she find us?"

"Daniel brought me," I said.

The woman's eyes narrowed at me. "Daniel Starr?"

Ginger laid a hand on the woman's shoulder. "Relax, Meg. He didn't hang around."

"He's lucky I don't have my wand on me," Meg grumbled.

"So what else does the coven do besides exercise?" I asked, hoping to distract Meg from Daniel's existence. She seemed to be as annoyed with him as Mayor Knightsbridge.

"Let's wait until we're sure you're one of us before we reveal our secrets," Meg said, eyeing me carefully.

"We need to babysit her until the council meeting," Ginger said. "Mayor's orders."

"The council is already freaking out about Gareth," Meg said. "This is going to tip them over the edge."

"The mayor mentioned Gareth was murdered," I said. "Who was he?"

"Spellbound's public defender," Meg said. "A pillar of the community."

"A fabulous guy," Ginger added. "He will be sorely missed."

The rest of the room murmured in agreement.

"Are murders typical around here?" I asked.

They exchanged looks. "They happen from time to time," Ginger said. "We're a community of supernaturals. When tempers flare, it's immediately dangerous."

My stomach twisted. I was stuck in a town with dangerous supernatural creatures where a road rage incident could turn deadly on a dime? Hang on, that sounded eerily like the human world.

Ginger studied me. "Are you hungry, honey? Why don't we take you for something to eat while we wait for Mayor Knightsbridge to take the wand out of her butt and convene the council."

"Ginger," Meg scolded her. "Felicity is the mayor. You can't talk about her like that." She lowered her voice. "At least not in front of the new girl. Take her to Perky's."

"No," Ginger said. "Let's go to Brew-Ha-Ha. They have more interesting shots."

"Shots?" I echoed.

"Don't worry," Ginger said. "We're not talking about alcohol. These are magical shots. For your latte."

More wonderful words had never been spoken. "That sounds amazing."

"Care to join us, big sister?" Ginger asked Meg.

"I'll finish up the class," Meg said. "One of us

needs to keep the weight off our bums." Meg twirled her finger in the air, a sign for the music to continue.

Ginger and I walked around the block to a coffee shop on the corner of the town square. It was a charming space with antique wooden tables and well-worn leather chairs.

"Fabulous," Ginger said. "Henrik is working today. He's the fastest barista there is."

I glanced behind the counter to see a middle-aged man with spiky hair and a face that suggested a fully lived life. "He's fast?" He looked like he'd rather be swinging in a hammock with a guitar and a bottle of beer.

Ginger wiggled her eyebrows at me. "Watch." She stepped up to the counter. "Morning, Henrik."

"Hey, sexy red witch." He nodded toward me. "Don't recognize you."

"She's a friend," Ginger said. "We'd like two lattes, one with a shot of unicorn horn and the other with a shot of empowerment."

Henrik's eyes bulged. "Going for the big stuff this early, huh? Got an important meeting?"

Ginger bumped me with her hip. "This one does."

She studied the food behind the glass. "And I'll have a wistberry muffin and she'll have a fill-me cake."

"What's a fill-me cake?" I asked quietly.

"It'll keep you going," Ginger said. "If the council meeting goes on for as long as I think it will, you'll be starving without something like this."

"Okay, thanks." I looked around the room for an empty table. There weren't many, given the early hour.

"There's a free booth." Ginger pointed across the room. By the time I turned back around, our entire order was ready.

"You weren't kidding," I said. "He is fast."

"Thanks, love," Henrik said.

We didn't need to carry a thing. They floated along beside us until we reached our table and then the items set themselves down in front of us.

"Amazing," I breathed.

"I bet you'll be saying that a lot here," Ginger predicted.

The cake and latte were delicious. The top of my latte was even decorated with a white heart in foam.

"How did he know?" I asked.

Ginger looked blank. "Know what?"

"My mom's last name was White and my dad's

was Hart." I showed her the inside of the mug. "Is he a wizard or something?"

"No, he's a berserker."

I wasn't sure what that was, but it sounded crazy.

"Everyone gets a heart on their latte. It's one of Henrik's signatures."

"Oh."

Something clattered to the floor beside my feet.

"There goes my wand," Ginger groaned. "Would you mind picking it up for me?"

A real witch's wand. I bent over and plucked the wand off the floor. It was prettier than I expected. Butter yellow with a brown leather band around the wider end.

I handed the wand back to Ginger.

"Thanks," she said, and tucked the wand in the back of her yoga pants.

A set of familiar pink wings fluttered between tables, heading our way.

"I think it might be time for me to go," I said.

Ginger craned her neck to see Lucy. "Finish up. If you're going before the council, you don't want to waste a drop of empowerment."

I tipped back the mug and sucked down every last drop. It was delicious. And empowering.

I hoped.

CHAPTER 3

THE COUNCIL CONVENED in a building aptly called the Great Hall. If my future weren't hanging in the balance, I would have taken pleasure in admiring the beautiful architecture. With its curved archways and marble floors, it was closer to a palace than an administrative building.

I sat alone on a bench in the grand lobby, waiting to be summoned. The plan seemed to be that they would decide my fate and then clue me in afterward.

Every few minutes I heard yelling and pounding from inside. My case appeared to be a contentious one. Not only were my palms sweating, but my chest and the back of my neck had joined the fun too. The council might decide to throw me to the werewolves based on my shattered appearance alone.

Finally the doors opened and Lucy flew out of

the closed chambers. She zipped over to me, her wings fluttering rapidly. She looked every inch as nervous as I did. At least I knew fairies could feel empathy. Maybe Mayor Knightsbridge would show the same degree of care.

"They're ready for you, Miss Hart."

I checked the clock on the nearby wall. Hours had passed since Lucy brought me here. I wondered if I'd have somewhere to sleep tonight. Not that it would happen easily. Anxiety kept me awake on a normal night and this was far from it.

She brought me to the oversized double doors. "I'd sprinkle fairy dust on you, but I don't have any on me."

I assumed that was a way of wishing me luck.

"I hope you get paid overtime," I said, and stepped inside.

I recognized the mayor from our earlier meeting, but that was the only familiar face. It felt like a congressional hearing, with the council members seated at a long table on an elevated dais. Lucy showed me wear to sit, although it was fairly obvious since it was the only available chair. An image of an electric chair flashed in my mind and my heart seized.

Seven sets of eyes watched me carefully as I took my seat.

Mayor Knightsbridge spoke first. "Miss Hart, welcome to the Great Hall of Spellbound. Allow me to introduce the council." She gestured to the male on her right. He was a stocky man with exaggerated facial features. "Wayne Stone is our resident number cruncher. In other words, he handles the budget. He's also an accountant, should you find yourself in need of one."

"He's a troll," Lucy whispered from behind me.

That explained the cave-dwelling vibe I got from him.

"Lorenzo Mancini is the leader of the werewolf pack," the mayor continued. "He's also a successful businessman in town."

I would have guessed werewolf for Lorenzo. He was exactly how I imagined a werewolf in human form would look. Dark, muscled, and oozing raw sensuality. He was dressed in an expensive-looking navy blue suit with a red tie. His gold cufflinks glittered in the artificial light.

My attention moved on to the man beside Mancini. With his pallid complexion and air of superiority, he had vampire written all over him.

"Lord Lewis Gilder is a highly respected member of the community," Mayor Knightsbridge said.

Lord Gilder lowered his head in acknowledgment and I found myself mirroring his movement. Was he exercising some kind of mind control? Was that allowed during an official procedure?

"Maeve McCullen is the owner and operator of Spellbound's premiere theater. If you enjoy live performances, it's well worth a visit."

"Banshee," Lucy whispered. I wasn't sure what a banshee was. I remembered a story from my childhood about a wailing spirit in Ireland who appeared whenever someone died, but I wasn't sure if that was accurate.

"And this is Juliet Montlake. She owns the local bookstore and is incredibly knowledgeable about the history of Spellbound and its variety of inhabitants. Should you have questions, she's a fine resource."

Juliet was tall with broad shoulders and thick chestnut-colored hair. She seemed the friendliest of the bunch.

"Amazon," Lucy said, ever helpful.

"And, finally, I would like to introduce Lady J.R. Weatherby, leader of the coven."

Lady Weatherby was an imposing figure, even

while seated. She wore a flowing white robe, a silver headdress with horns curving upward, and a red statement necklace around her throat. Her dark hair hung loose along her shoulders. She reminded me of Cleopatra.

Lady Weatherby glowered at me from beneath the twisted horns of her headdress and the hair on the back of my neck prickled.

"Now to the business at hand," Mayor Knightsbridge said. "I'm sure you have many questions about the town and how we came to be contained here."

Contained. An interesting choice of words.

Maeve poked her head forward and faced the mayor. "If I may, Madam Mayor."

"Yes, please do," Mayor Knightsbridge said. "Maeve always tells the story best."

Maeve stood, her strawberry blond ringlets bouncing around her shoulders. "Once upon a time, there was a lovely town called Ridge Valley where supernaturals came and went as they pleased."

"There are towns full of supernaturals all over the world," Wayne interjected. "They're hidden from human sight."

So Spellbound wasn't the only one. Wow. Mind blown.

"One day," Maeve continued, in an animated voice entirely suitable for the stage, "an enchantress arrived in town in the guise of an ugly old woman, seeking shelter from a storm. The legend states that, although she knocked on many doors that night, none were opened to her. Enraged, she cursed the town, making sure that the residents of Ridge Valley would never be able to leave its borders and spread their selfishness and greed to other towns."

"It is only a legend, mind you," Lord Gilder stated. "No one knows for certain."

"Another story suggests that her heart was broken by someone in the town," Juliet said, "and she cursed the borders so he could never leave, but the curse ended up trapping the rest of the inhabitants as well."

"Eventually," Maeve said, "Ridge Valley became known as Spellbound." She spread her arms. "And here we remain."

And I thought I was unlucky.

Mayor Knightsbridge addressed me. "Do you have any questions so far, Miss Hart?"

How much time did they have?

"Why does no one know for certain?" I asked. "Weren't you all here when it happened?" The beings seemed to be either immortal or ones with very long life spans.

"Not all of us," the mayor said. "Several generations have been born here since the curse."

"And those of us old enough to have been here at the time of the enchantress," Lord Gilder interrupted, "do not know or recall the particulars of the event. One day we could leave at will, and then we could not."

"Is there a way to break the curse?" I asked. The town was full of witches and fairies. Surely they had skills comparable to an enchantress.

"Not that we've found so far or we wouldn't be here, would we?" the mayor said.

"So it's basically a magical Guantanamo," I said.

"Pardon?" the mayor said.

Clearly she wasn't familiar with the U.S. detention camp.

"Okay, maybe more like Phantom Zone," I said. "You know, the prison dimension in Superman."

Mayor Knightsbridge narrowed her eyes. "I don't understand the words you're saying."

I tried again. "Azkaban?"

She sighed and rolled her eyes. "That's a book, dear. Fictional."

"Are you equating Spellbound with Tartarus?" Juliet asked.

I recognized that name from the Greek myths. It was the place where wicked people were sent to live the rest of their lives in suffering and torment.

"She wouldn't dare," Mayor Knightsbridge said with a dismissive flick of her fingers. "That place is a pit of despair. We have all the modern conveniences."

All the modern conveniences? They didn't appear to have television or the internet. What did she consider modern—indoor plumbing?

"Ooh," Maeve said, bouncing in her seat a little. "I've got one. Perhaps we're like Australia but without the koalas."

"No," Wayne said. "Remember Hester has a koala."

"I believe we're getting off track," the mayor said. The gavel in front of her lifted and banged on the sound block without anyone touching it.

She was right. I gathered my courage and spoke. "So what's going to happen to me? Am I able to leave?"

Mayor Knightsbridge steepled her fingers. "No, dear. It simply isn't possible."

"Because I'm...I'm one of you?" The reality hadn't settled in yet. I wasn't sure if it ever would.

"You are a witch," Lady Weatherby said. "We confirmed it before you arrived for this meeting."

"Confirmed it how?" I asked.

"The latte you drank earlier included a potion called Reveal," Lady Weatherby explained. "Ginger slipped it in when you weren't looking. She's a rather accomplished witch for someone of her age."

"How does it reveal that I'm a witch?" I asked. "Is there a report somewhere?"

Lady Weatherby suppressed a smile. "*You* are the report, Miss Hart. If the person who drinks the potion glows purple, then she is a witch."

"You've been glowing purple since you left Brew-Ha-Ha," Lucy whispered behind me.

I held out my hands in front of me. Sure enough, I detected a purplish haze.

"But this isn't possible," I said, trying to rub the purple off my hands. "I would have known."

"Whether you knew it or not is irrelevant," Lady Weatherby said. "You will learn witchcraft like every young witch in the coven."

Learn witchcraft? "You mean you're going to send me to school?" Between college and law school,

I'd had quite enough formal education, thank you very much.

"The Arabella St. Simon Academy for Witches is an excellent institution," Lady Weatherby said.

"The ASS Academy?" I asked, gobsmacked. "You cannot be serious."

Lady Weatherby fixed me with her hard stare and I involuntarily shuddered. "I am as serious as a headstone."

Okay, a headstone sounded pretty serious.

"Where will I live?" I asked. "Is there a dormitory?" The thought of bunking with a room full of younger witches set my teeth on edge.

The council sat in collective silence.

Finally Lady Weatherby spoke. "She won't be permitted to live with the coven until she's completed her training. Standard protocol." She faced me. "Younger witches usually live at home during their early education."

And I was homeless.

"There is an available house…" Maeve trailed off, afraid to finish the thought.

Everyone's eyes widened.

"It does make the most sense," Lord Gilder said. "The place will sit empty otherwise. Gareth didn't have any heirs. His property will simply revert to the town."

"She'll need to pay rent," Wayne said. "She can't live off the town for free."

"Never mind the money right now." The mayor looked thoughtful. "She claims to have been a lawyer in the human world."

All eyes turned back to me.

"We do need an urgent replacement for Gareth," Lorenzo said. "He was in the middle of a trial. Mumford has been quite upset about the whole affair. He wants the trial over and done with."

"I don't blame him," Wayne said. "The case against him is flimsy at best."

"Um, excuse me," I said, raising my hand. "But I don't know the first thing about being a criminal defense attorney."

"You know how to stand in front of a judge, don't you?" the mayor asked.

"Yes, but..."

"And you know how to recite the relevant law?" Wayne asked.

"Yes, but that doesn't..."

"Congratulations, Miss Hart," the mayor said. "You're Spellbound's new public defender."

"She'll need to fit her work in between classes," Lady Weatherby said. "Her education in witchcraft is essential. We can't have untrained witches running amok in Spellbound. It will reflect poorly on the coven."

"I'm sure that can be arranged," Mayor Knightsbridge said. "Lucy, you'll escort Miss Hart to her new home, won't you?"

"Yes, Madam Mayor." Lucy beamed like she'd been awarded top prize in a beauty pageant.

I gave Lucy a curious glance. "You really love your job, don't you?"

She laughed giddily. "I have the best job in the world. What's not to love?"

"The key is under the gargoyle," Lord Gilder added. "Be prepared, Miss Hart. You have rather big shoes to fill."

"Speaking of shoes," Mayor Knightsbridge said. "Lucy, please be sure to find Miss Hart a pair of matching socks."

If I hadn't already been glowing purple, I would have turned bright red.

When Lucy excused herself to use the restroom before taking me to Gareth's house, I made a break for it. It wasn't a conscious decision. I simply felt my feet moving out of the Great Hall and across town before I could stop myself.

I couldn't wrap my head around everything that was happening. Part of me was still convinced it was a dream. How could I be a witch? How could I live twenty-five years of my life and not know I was a witch? Then again, I didn't have my parents growing up. If I was descended from witches on my mother's side, then that explained the knowledge gap. Did my mother know she was a witch? I knew nothing about her parents. Other than that they were dead. They died before I was even born.

I followed the path out of town, the one where Daniel had first taken me. I thought it was worth having another look to see whether there was something we missed. Maybe it was all a huge mistake.

The trees grew taller, wider, and more frequent as I walked. Under different circumstances, I would have found this town enchanting. A place where you would go on holiday and tell your friends about it later. Post three hundred pictures on Facebook to make everyone jealous. But I had to see this place differently now. I had to see it as my new home. I would never see my apartment again. It wasn't such a great apartment, but it was still where I lived. It was my home. True, I had no family to miss me, but surely someone would. I pondered the list of potential people. It wasn't a very long one, sadly. I mostly kept to myself. I did my job, met with clients, paid my bills on time, and basically went about my day.

I stood in front of the two white birch trees. Would anything be different if I tried to leave now? Maybe there had been a glitch like with computers. I bet magic went awry sometimes, like technology. Nothing was perfect.

I took another step closer. And then another. When I stepped again, the tip of my big toe hit that invisible wall. Well, that was going to bruise. I took a few steps backward. What if I gave a running start? Maybe the speed was an issue. I could burst through the invisible barrier if I just gained enough momentum.

I walked back about twenty paces and turned to face the trees again. I tried to remember the position a sprinter took at the beginning of a race. I hunched over and pressed my fingertips to the ground.

"I wouldn't do that if I were you," a familiar voice said. Daniel.

"Are you following me?" I asked. "Because I don't think I need a guardian angel anymore."

"Oh, but I think you do. You're about to give

yourself a concussion. That is not the action of a sane person."

My cheeks reddened. "I was not going to give myself a concussion," I insisted.

He spread his arms wide. "You can test the entire length of the border. I promise you, you can't get out. Over the years, I have tested every inch of the barrier. The magic is firmly intact."

"How can the enchantress have cursed the whole town and then left you here to rot?" I asked. "Even if she had been mistreated, it seems harsh to leave the inhabitants and their offspring cursed for eternity. The younger generations are innocent."

Daniel shrugged. "Our world can be cruel and indifferent like yours," he said. "Just different methods."

"Do you remember her?" I asked. "The enchantress."

His expression darkened. "I don't want to talk about the curse. It's ancient history."

"It seems very present for all of you," I said. "And now for me." I studied him for a moment, the knowledge stirring in my heart. "You really weren't just thinking up on that clifftop, were you?"

"Of course I was. I told you. That's my safe spot to think."

"To think about killing yourself," I said softly. Looking at him now, I was certain of it. "I'll bet you were going to jump. Keep your wings closed and plummet into the water. I'll bet you can't swim because of the wings." They'd drag him down like bricks tied to his back.

His jaw tensed. "I thought you were a lawyer in the human world, not a psychoanalyst."

"You know a lot about my world considering you've been stuck here forever and a day."

"We're not completely cut off from information. There are ways of keeping tabs if you're so inclined."

I'd need to ask more about that. If there was a way of keeping up with my favorite television shows, I was totally on board with that. Bring on the magical Netflix.

"You're an angel," I said. "How could your existence here be so terrible that you'd want to end it all?"

"I told you..." he began, and then his features suddenly softened. "Okay, fine. You know what? I feel like being honest with you. You're right. I'd heard the news about Gareth and I realized that I wasn't sad like I should have been. I was jealous. He had gotten out, yet I was still here. For eternity. I couldn't bear the thought for a minute more."

"Is the town so awful?" I asked. "I mean, I didn't exactly make plans to relocate here, but it seems like an amazing place."

"Enjoying it so much that you came here to escape?" He gave me a gentle smile.

"I'm freaked out right now. Otherwise, I'd really be enjoying it."

He raked a hand through his blond hair. "Do you think you'll be saying that after a hundred years or so?"

"I don't know yet," I said. "I guess ask me in a hundred years." I mustered a smile.

"If it makes you feel any better," he said, "I'm not considering it anymore. I've been doing a little soul-searching and I feel the fog lifting."

I wondered if he spent less time up his own ass, if he'd be any less emo.

"I heard you need to start classes at the witch academy," he said. "I know Lady Weatherby can be a little intimidating."

"A little?" I'd come up against a lot of surly judges in my professional career, but not one of them made me quake in my boots the way Lady Weatherby did.

"Look on the bright side," Daniel said. "It must be exciting for you to realize you have powers you didn't even know about. Humans love that stuff."

"I'm sure if I were any good at...well, anything, I'd be over the moon. I'm pretty sure I won't be able to live up to Lady Weatherby's exacting standards."

He patted my back. "Give it time, Emma. You've only just arrived. Things will get better."

"Says the angel contemplating suicide."

He narrowed his eyes at me. "Let's not speak of it again. Agreed?"

"As long as you don't tell anyone about me making a run for the border." God, I even missed Taco Bell. Maybe it was PMS talking.

"How about I take you home?" he said.

"Only if we can walk," I replied. "I don't think I can handle another flight so soon."

He held out his hand and smiled. "Then let's walk."

CHAPTER 4

WE ONLY MADE it as far as the first set of buildings in town when Lucy found me.

"There you are," she said cheerfully, as though she'd misplaced me. "We should go and get you settled in for the night."

Reluctantly, I released Daniel's hand. "I'll see you around town, I guess."

"Definitely."

He flew off in a blaze of white wings, and I forced my attention back to Lucy. "How far is it?"

She pulled out her wand. "Don't worry about those delicate feet of yours. I'm going to sprinkle you with fairy dust. Mayor Knightsbridge lent me a packet of hers."

"Wait," I said, and held out my hands to repel the sparkling magic powder. Too late.

My feet lifted off the ground and I began to float. Lucy grasped my hand, giggling, and fluttered her wings.

"I'm not strong enough to carry you," she said, "but I can guide you there with a little help."

I'm not going to lie. I threw up somewhere over a pasture. I was just relieved it didn't land on someone's house. Lucy was polite enough not to mention it.

Gareth's house was located in the northwest corner on the outskirts of town. Lucy's small, pink wings slowed and we floated down to the ground.

The house was a large Victorian with beautiful stained glass windows. Two red Adirondack chairs were carefully arranged on the wraparound front porch.

"It's lovely," I said. Much nicer than any home I'd ever lived in. My current apartment was about six hundred square feet with shag carpet and a bathroom suite the shade of avocado.

"You'll probably want to make some alterations," Lucy said, and lifted the base of the gargoyle at the bottom of the steps. A chunky silver key appeared in her hand. We walked onto the front porch where she unlocked the door and pushed it open.

"I'm sure it's perfect as it is," I said. Aside from the gargoyle. I'd definitely get rid of that.

The second I stepped into the entryway, I longed to snatch back the words. Although the outside was charming, the inside appeared to have been decorated by a goth. Dark purple paint stained the walls and blackout curtains obscured the gorgeous windows.

"What was wrong with Gareth?" I asked. "Was he some kind of hermit?" And, if so, how did he manage to get himself murdered?

"No, silly," Lucy said. "Gareth was a vampire."

A shiver ran down my spine. I was going to inhabit the home of a vampire?

"The public defender was a vampire?" I queried.

"Yes. And Lord Gilder sits on the council. We have a healthy and thriving vampire community here in Spellbound."

A healthy and thriving vampire community? Was that because they had open access to veins in this town?

Lucy must have read my mind because she added, "Not to worry. Vampires own the Blood Bank. It's a cooperative venture. They get all the blood they need from there."

A vampire co-op. How progressive.

"I think you're right. A little renovation work will be in order," I said. Dark colors aside, the interior seemed a bit neglected. A banister with chipped black paint and a missing support post, half a stair runner, and threadbare rugs.

"Goodness me," Lucy exclaimed. "No one noticed the embers still burning in the fireplace?"

I was surprised he used the fireplace at all since it was about seventy degrees outside. Then again, he was a vampire, so I guess poor circulation was an issue for him.

She fluttered into the adjoining room where an enormous fireplace took center stage. The mantel appeared to be made of concrete and adorned with scrolls. It was the kind of mantel that cried out for Christmas decorations. Despite my nervousness, I felt a little rise of excitement at the prospect of decorating a house like this.

Lucy produced her glittery wand and snuffed out the remaining orange glow. "That's better. We wouldn't want this lovely house to burn to the ground now, would we?"

The term lovely was debatable. Other than that, I agreed with her.

"I take it Gareth wasn't into decorating."

"Oh, he had wonderful style," she said. "But I

don't think he spent much time on this floor of the house. You'll probably find other areas of the home less neglected."

I sure hoped so. I began to count the cobwebs in the living room but stopped when I reached double digits.

"Do you know anything about the case he was working on before he died?" I asked.

"Yes, everybody knows. He was defending a goblin called Mumford. He's been accused of stealing jewelry from the dwarves."

"Do dwarves wear a lot of jewelry?" I asked. It was hard to imagine fat, hairy men decked out in sparkling gemstones, but I wasn't one to judge.

"No, silly. Dwarves are master craftsmen. They mine the gems and make the jewelry by hand. They're famous for it. Deacon's store in town is very popular. That's where the jewels were stolen from."

"What's the evidence?" I asked.

"I don't know the details, but I believe they found a loose diamond in Mumford's pocket. The rest of the jewelry is still missing."

"Where does Mumford say he got the diamond?"

"He says he found it on the road on the way into town. That the real thief must have dropped it during his escape."

It was plausible, especially if they hadn't managed to locate the rest of the stolen items.

"How was Gareth killed?" If he was a vampire, I had to imagine it had not been easy.

"He was staked." She shuddered. "They found him on a bed of leaves in the forest. The sheriff hasn't found the murder weapon, though."

"So you're looking for a piece of wood in the woods?" Talk about a needle in a haystack.

"The sheriff and his deputy have been searching high and low. I have every confidence they'll find it." Her enthusiasm seemed entirely genuine. It was both sweet and disconcerting.

"Why don't you show me the rest of the house?" I suggested.

Lucy giggled. "This is so fun. I would have been a realtor if Mayor Knightsbridge hadn't hired me."

I followed her back to the depressing staircase and we headed downstairs. "There's a basement?"

"Not quite," she said.

Not quite was correct. The entire downstairs level was Gareth's master bedroom. There was a glossy black coffin on a raised platform in the middle of the room with a shiny disco ball hanging directly above it. The interior of the coffin appeared to be made of white silk.

"This is...not what I expected," I said. How could downstairs Gareth be the same as upstairs Gareth?

"It's an amazing space," Lucy said. "Except for the lack of natural light, of course. But you can use the bedrooms upstairs. There's no reason for you to use this room as your own."

No, I probably—definitely—wouldn't.

"Lord Gilder was outside during the day," I said. Unless there were underground passages that led to the Great Hall. "Can vampires walk around in daylight here?"

"They can," Lucy said. "The paranormal towns have a special atmospheric layer that protects vampires from the sun. They still prefer darkness, however. It's more natural for them."

"Is that a closet?" I asked, pointing across the room.

"Yes. It looks like that whole wall is lined with closet space."

Wow. This room was bigger than my apartment and my neighbor's apartment combined.

"You know, I only have the outfit I came in," I said. "Is there any way I can get clothes and pajamas?" And matching socks, of course. As a fairy, I thought Lucy might be able to bibbety bobbety some clothes for me.

"Absolutely. In fact, Mayor Knightsbridge has instructed me to take you shopping tomorrow."

"That's kind of her."

"We'll just take it out of the emergency budget." She laughed gaily. "After all, that's what it's for. Emergencies."

"I'll need toiletries too," I said. In fact, I would need every basic necessity. An image of my white bunny slippers flashed in my mind and I ached with longing. I knew I was too old for them, but I didn't care. No one ever saw me at bedtime anyway. It wasn't like I had a boyfriend staying over or anyone dropping by unannounced. That was one of the upsides of not having a family. They couldn't annoy me with unexpected visits, or other kinds of behavior people with loved ones complained about.

Lucy linked her arm through mine. "Not to worry, Miss Hart. We'll get you all set up so you can get to work on your very first case."

And start witch training. And I thought my old life was stressful. I had a feeling that Spellbound was about to take stress and anxiety to a whole new level.

The next morning, the sound of a horn jolted me to my feet. I peered out the front door to see Lucy seated in the driver's seat of a bright orange jalopy. It reminded me of a Ford Model T but with more sparkles.

"What does this thing run on?" I asked, climbing into the passenger seat. The dashboard made no sense to me at all. It didn't include any of the usual 'ometers and interior fixtures.

"Magical energy, of course," Lucy said. "The town is full of it."

"And you harness it to run your vehicles?"

"Basically."

I thought about my own beloved car at the bottom of Swan Lake. "How fast can this go?" It looked like it might fall apart over forty miles per hour.

Lucy wiggled her eyebrows. "Let's find out." She pressed a button rather than a pedal and we lurched forward.

As I gripped the dashboard and gritted my teeth, I swear I experienced a temporary facelift.

"Okay, the answer is fast," I managed to squeak.

She slowed to a normal pace. "That was fun."

"Are you sure you're not a demon?" I asked.

"Only in the bedroom, Miss Hart," she said with a wink.

"Do you have the expression TMI here?" I asked.

"If not, I'll be sure to introduce it into the Spellbound vernacular."

Lucy hopped excitedly in her seat. "Where shall we go first? Clothes shopping?"

"A few outfits would probably be a good idea," I said. Although I'd showered in Gareth's oversized bathroom, I still wore the same clothes I'd arrived in. I'd slept naked just to give my clothes a break.

We passed by an enormous row of shrubs. "What's that?"

"You should definitely check it out when you get a chance. It's an elaborate maze designed by our resident minotaur, Markos. He also runs a children's bouncy house maze across town." She gave me a pointed look. "He does very well for himself"—she lowered her voice—"and he's hung like a...well, like a minotaur."

Having witnessed plenty of Lucy's sweet side, I now seemed to be getting a glimpse of the fairy's saucy side.

"If he's such a catch, why don't you go out with him?" I asked.

"He's not into wings," she said sadly. "At least you've got a chance."

"I'm good, thanks."

Lucy pulled into a parking lot on a side street

near the town square. "There are heaps of places within walking distance from here."

We left the parking lot and I caught sight of the largest, most impressive fountain I'd ever seen. It easily could have doubled as a lake. There were twelve statues of dolphins and mermaids around the perimeter and the water spouted ten feet into the air.

"It's pretty, isn't it?" Lucy asked, noting the object of my attention. "The naiads do an amazing job. You should definitely hire them if you ever decide to put in a pool."

A pool. The suggestion made my presence here sound so permanent. Even though I knew that it was, part of me still clung to the belief that this was a temporary mistake that would get straightened out. Eventually.

We passed a shop window with a huge heart etched in the glass. "That's Pandora's matchmaking office. She's a nymph. If you decide you'd like to meet that special someone, she can help. She also runs a speed dating night on Thursdays. I've been a few times. It's a lot of fun."

I had no plans for speed dating here, or dating of any kind. I found human dating stressful enough.

"Oh, look. There's the big boss." Lucy beamed at

the sight of Mayor Knightsbridge. The blue-winged fairy strode toward us on the cobblestone, flanked by two large hounds.

"What kind of dogs are they?" I asked.

"Hellhounds," Lucy replied matter-of-factly. "Just don't pet the wrong one or you might lose a hand."

The wrong one? They looked identical. Which one was the wrong one?

"Lucy, I'm so pleased to see you've taken our new resident under your wing. Are you enjoying the town, Miss Hart?"

"It's wonderful," I said, keeping one eye trained on the hellhounds. "Are these your security detail?"

Mayor Knightsbridge chuckled. "In a manner of speaking, I suppose. Zeus is to my right. He still thinks he's a puppy. Chases squirrels and likes belly rubs. Hera is a real bitch." She glanced at the hound on her left. "Trouble is they look alike, so you must take care when approaching them."

Note to self: no belly rubs for hellhounds. Not worth the risk to life and limb.

"You should take her to Ricardo's shop," Mayor Knightsbridge said. "He's running a huge sale at the moment."

"We're on the way there now," Lucy said.

"Excellent. I'll see you at the mansion later, Lucy." She gave me a crisp nod before carrying on.

"Is Ricardo a fairy, too?" I asked.

"No, he's a wereferret with impeccable taste." She looped her arm through mine. "I'm excited about the sale. He only runs them occasionally."

We rounded the corner and I recognized the town square and the clock tower. The shop was called, aptly enough, Ready-to-Were.

Ricardo rushed forward to greet us, kissing Lucy on both cheeks. "You are a vision, as always, Miss Lucy."

Wearing bright turquoise trousers and a fuchsia and turquoise striped shirt, Ricardo was quite a vision as well. I wasn't sure what I expected a wereferret to look like, but Ricardo certainly wasn't it.

"Ricardo, I'd like you to meet Miss Emma Hart, Spellbound's new witch."

When he leaned forward to kiss my cheek, I stuck out my hand. "Nice to meet you."

"You witches are all the same," he said with a friendly laugh.

Since when were handshakes a witch thing? I just wasn't keen on the idea of a wereferret's saliva on my skin. Yikes, that sounded racist even in my head.

I was going to need an attitude adjustment if I was going to fit in here.

Lucy was right about Ricardo's taste, though. The shop was full of gorgeous clothing in all cuts and colors. There were no sizes. If you liked something, you tried it on and it automatically catered to your body. Nothing ever had to be tailored to fit. It was easily the best thing about Spellbound so far, aside from the coffee.

I stood in front of a mirror and studied my reflection. This was the fourth outfit I'd tried on and it looked just as amazing as the first three. That had never happened to me in the human world. I'd always needed the same tops and bottoms in multiple sizes because I never knew what would fit. And even when it fit, that didn't mean it looked good on me.

"Are you sure this isn't a magic mirror?" I asked. I had images of me walking around town in one of these outfits and quickly discovering the attractive cut was an illusion.

"No magic mirrors in here, Miss Emma," Ricardo assured me. "Our clothing is carefully selected from the best magical manufacturers."

I was in heaven. "How many am I allowed to

have?" I asked Lucy. She hadn't told me what the budget was.

"With a sale this good, get as many outfits as you like," Lucy said.

"We'll be changing over to a new collection soon," Ricardo explained. "We need to move inventory."

Then this was my lucky day—and I never had lucky days.

Once the clothes were paid for, I turned to Lucy. "Should we lug these back to the car?"

"Don't be silly," she said. "They'll be in your closet when you get home."

My eyes popped. "What? How?"

Ricardo grinned. "It's fun having someone new in town, no?"

Lucy clapped her hands. "It really is."

"You should take her to the Wish Market," Ricardo said. "I'll bet she's never seen anything like that."

Ricardo wasn't kidding.

The market was unreal. It was an outdoor shopping area tucked down a side street parallel to the town square. There were stalls filled with unusual food and drinks. Above the stalls were floating shelves piled with handmade hats, scarves, and other small items.

"Take a basket," Lucy urged, and I picked up a woven basket from the table beside the entrance.

"How can I possibly reach the top shelves?" I asked. "I don't have wings like you."

"There's no need," Lucy said. "You simply think of it and it appears in your basket. Like this." She closed her eyes and I watched in awe as a bag of bright purple apples appeared in the basket. Well, they were the shape of apples anyway.

"That's incredible," I breathed. "Everything looks so good. I don't even know where to start." I loved food. I wasn't so great at cooking it, but I definitely loved to eat it.

"Let's walk down the main strip and, whenever you see something you like the look of, just wish it into your basket."

"Now I understand why it's called the Wish Market."

I loaded up on everything that screamed 'eat me.' I had no idea how to prepare any of it, but I didn't care. I was having too much fun. Lucy was the perfect companion for a day like this. She seemed to delight in my enjoyment.

"I'm going to need a cookbook or something," I said, as we headed back to the car.

"There are a few excellent ones in the bookstore," Lucy said. "We'll stop there another time. We want the food sent to your house before it spoils."

As Lucy revved the magical engine, an impatient driver began honking incessantly. "I'm not going to move any faster because you're honking at me," she muttered.

We proceeded to sit there while the other car horn went ballistic.

"What are we doing?" I asked.

Lucy folded her arms. "Sitting here longer for no reason, obviously. I'm not letting that harpy get her way."

"Why not?" I asked. "She's obviously in a hurry."

Lucy smiled. "Exactly."

Now that I had clean underwear and matching socks, I turned my attention to the house. Its size was overwhelming—about ten times the size of my apartment. Although certain rooms were a little creepy, I knew they could be beautiful with the right touches. A house like this in eastern Pennsylvania would cost far more than I could've ever afforded on the salary of a public interest lawyer.

I decided to explore Gareth's study today. I thought it would be a good opportunity to see if he brought his work home with him. Maybe there were files here that he didn't keep at the office in town and I could brush up on Mumford's case.

I located his study on the main floor in the west wing. The room was, of course, enormous. With its high ceilings and intricate woodwork, I could imagine this room as it may have once been used. Maybe a ballroom or a drawing room with ladies in gowns. Despite the dismal paint colors, the room still held astounding beauty. The colorful stained glass windows only added to its appeal. I looked around in wonder. This was actually going to be my home office. It was a far cry from a laptop on the sofa in front of the television.

I walked over to the desk. It appeared to be made from reclaimed wood. An interesting choice for a vampire. Surprising that he would have wanted to surround himself with so much wood. On the other hand, he'd left the home's original features intact. Maybe because he appreciated all that this house had to offer. Looking around, I had the overwhelming feeling I would have liked him.

I sat down in the chair and began examining the contents of the folders on the desk. It felt odd not to be opening a laptop. I would have to get used to the lack of technology. It didn't seem to bother anyone else. Then again, they didn't have the same experience with technology that I did. Like most people I knew, I'd come to depend on it.

I flipped through the papers in the first file. A trespassing case against a werewolf. That case closed a few weeks ago. I had to admit, the idea of a werewolf traipsing across my lawn in the middle of the night made me feel a little uneasy. I looked to see who the claimant was. Someone named Calliope Minor. Calliope sounded familiar. I was fairly sure she was one of my neighbors. I shuddered. So there was a very good chance a werewolf might decide that my yard made a good shortcut. They probably wouldn't dream of cutting across a vampire's yard. Now that an inexperienced witch had moved in, all bets were off.

I opened the next folder. A shoplifting case. An elf called Chip was caught stealing sweets from Taffy's. A candy shop presumably. A long explanation was included as to why he had taken the sweets. I opened a third file. This one did not include a case.

I studied the paper more closely. It had been

drafted by Gareth himself. A petition to have holy water removed from the church. He argued that its use was discriminatory and created a health and safety issue for vampires. I set down the paper and thought about it. Were vampires going to church in Spellbound? If not, then why did Gareth care whether there was holy water inside the church? I checked the file for any other relevant names. This looked like a recent project.

To my left, papers scattered to the floor, startling me. I whipped around to see a cat standing on a tabletop. I wasn't a huge fan of cats. I always had the irrational fear that I'd wake up to find one standing on my chest and sucking out my soul. Too many horror movies as a kid.

"Hello there," I said, forcing an unconcerned tone. "No one mentioned that Gareth had a cat. Are you supposed to be here?"

The cat hissed at me. It was—to be blunt—an ugly cat, hairless with an angry face and a half-chewed ear. I couldn't even tell what color it was supposed to be.

"You must be hungry," I said. "If you did belong to Gareth, then that means no one's been feeding you."

I left the file on the desk and walked down the corridor to the kitchen. The cat trailed after me, meowing incessantly. It wasn't a pleasant sound like the cats I'd seen in YouTube videos. It was more of an urgent screech.

"Don't rush me now. Just because you've decided to come out of the woodwork." I began opening cabinets in the kitchen to see if I could find any cat food. I hadn't noticed evidence of it before. Not that Gareth had much in the way of dried goods. His refrigerator was stocked full of bottles of blood, but not much else.

In the walk-in pantry, I found what I was looking for. Rows of cat food cans. "Someone's a fan of tuna."

I plucked a can from the shelf and rummaged through the drawers for a can opener. All the while the cat moved in and out of my legs. A trip hazard. He'd decided he was really hungry now and wasn't going to let me forget it.

I located a small dish and emptied the can into it. I had no clue how much to feed a cat. I set down the dish on the floor and watched the cat devour it. I felt a pang of sympathy for him. I found another dish and filled it with water, setting it beside the food.

"I'm so sorry, Mr. Cat." We'd only just met. It seemed too informal to call him anything else. "I wish you had let me know sooner you were here."

To be honest, the cat creeped me out. It wasn't

cute and fluffy like the ones in posters with motivational sayings. This one looked straight out of the insane asylum.

I made a mental note to find out if anyone was interested in taking on a pet. Maybe one of Gareth's friends. I would hunt down a new owner as soon as the opportunity presented itself. Unfortunately, I had no idea when that would be. I was due to start witch classes tomorrow morning. Between classes and my new job, I was going to struggle to find free time.

I glanced down at the cat, finishing up the bowl of water. "I guess it's you and me for a while."

Mr. Cat looked up at me and hissed.

"Right back at you," I said, and stuck out my tongue.

CHAPTER 5

THE CLASSROOM at ASS Academy reminded me of a chemistry lab. There were bubbling beakers of various colors, and long, perfunctory tables with stools in front of them. Four young women sat on the stools. The youngest looked to be about thirteen.

"You must be the new witch," the youngest one said. "My name is Laurel."

"Nice to meet you, Laurel," I said, although I'd never get used to being called a witch. It still sounded like an insult. "My name is..."

"Emma Hart," Laurel finished for me. "We know. It's all anyone can talk about."

I guess I wasn't surprised that my sudden appearance had made the local gossip rounds. "So what kind of class is this?"

"Beginner Spell Casting," Laurel said. "We also do Beginner Potions and Basic Skills."

I didn't ask what Basic Skills included—deciding where to place my wart for maximum impact?

"So are you all new witches, too?" I asked the others.

They exchanged uneasy glances.

"We are what you might call the remedial class," another witch said. "I'm Millie, by the way. And this is Begonia and Sophie."

"So why are you in the remedial class?" I asked.

"Because we haven't managed to pass all the tests," Begonia said. "Each time you fail, you have to start all over again."

"That seems a bit harsh," I said.

"Not when you're dealing with such powerful magic," Sophie replied. "If we're not proficient, we could hurt someone."

"Who's the instructor?" I asked. "Maybe she's not doing such a hot job."

Laurel giggled. "I wouldn't say that to her face. You might end up with a horrific rash."

"On your face," Sophie added.

"She's the head witch," Millie explained. "Lady J.R. Weatherby."

"Lady Weatherby?" I repeated. She'd been a member of the council in the Great Hall.

"That's her," Begonia said. "If you didn't know her by name, you can usually identify her by the scowl on her face."

"Yes, I got the impression she wasn't the warmest coal in the fire." More like the tundra.

"She's very tough," Millie whispered. "You don't want to get on her bad side."

I had no intention of getting on anyone's bad side in Spellbound. Any number of them could roast me and toast me with the flick of a finger.

"Glad to see you're all on time for a change." Lady Weatherby swept into the room and everyone stood perfectly still.

"Yes, Lady Weatherby," they murmured in unison.

She took her place in front of the class and glowered in my direction. "I trust you've all met the new student, Miss Hart."

"Thank you so much for having me," I said. "I really..."

"I have not asked you a question, Miss Hart," Lady Weatherby said.

Laurel leaned over and whispered. "We only speak in response to a question."

Oh. Like standing in front of a judge, in a way. I could do that.

"Today we will be reviewing the basic defensive spells. For the sake of our new student, can someone please refresh our memories as to what these are?"

Four hands shot up eagerly.

"Begonia."

Begonia's straightened her back and grinned broadly. "The four basic defensive spells are: the Blowback; the Spasm; the Sleeping Beauty; and the Shield."

"And which one of you would like to demonstrate?"

Four hands shot up again. For a remedial class, they seemed to have their act together. I wondered what the issue was.

"Sophie, please step up to the front of the class." Lady Weatherby's stark gaze settled on me. "And Miss Hart, you will assist her."

I wasn't sure how I could assist Sophie since I knew nothing about casting spells, but I followed her to the front of the class all the same.

"Stand about ten feet apart, please," Lady Weatherby said. "Start with Sleeping Beauty."

I suddenly felt like the boy with an apple on my

head. What was his name? William Tell? No, that was the father's name. The son was called Robert.

Sophie produced her wand and took aim. I closed my eyes in anticipation.

"I've had my fill/sleep you will."

Nothing happened. I popped one eye open to see Sophie snoring loudly on the floor.

"Can anyone with working eyesight tell me what Sophie did wrong?" Lady Weatherby asked.

Three hands shot up.

"Laurel?"

"She was holding her wand backwards," Laurel said.

"Very good."

Lady Weatherby snapped her fingers and Sophie awoke on the floor. She rubbed her eyes and glanced around the room.

"I did it again, didn't I?" she asked, rising to her feet.

Four heads nodded.

"Remember, Sophie," Lady Weatherby said. "The narrow end gets pointed at the object of the spell. You hold the broader end."

Sophie stared at her wand, tears brimming in her eyes. "There's not much difference."

"Maybe she needs a piece of colored tape around

the base of her wand," I said. "Then she can remember which end is the one she holds." When I was younger, I took piano lessons and my instructor labeled the keys with coded colors to help me learn faster. I'd found it very helpful.

Everyone looked at me. Sophie actually winced.

Lady Weatherby narrowed her eyes at me. "Miss Hart, need I remind you that no one asked you a question."

I clamped my mouth closed.

"Sophie, the Spasm spell," Lady Weatherby ordered, and I noticed the hint of a smile on her face.

Sophie took care in pointing the correct end of her wand at me. "Letter and stamp/give her a cramp."

My stomach seized and I doubled over, groaning in pain. It felt like the beginning stage of an acute case of Montezuma's Revenge.

Lady Weatherby snapped her fingers and the pain subsided. I stood erect and rubbed my stomach.

"Sorry," Sophie mouthed quietly.

I raised my hand this time. "Lady Weatherby?"

Her mouth formed a thin line. "Yes, Miss Hart?"

"Do you always say these little rhymes for the spells?" I asked.

"You are free to use these, or to make up one of

your own. It is the combination of the witch's will, her wand, and the incantation taken as a whole that makes the spell effective."

I was already imagining the infinite potential for rhymes. As a child, I'd loved nursery rhymes, although my grandparents weren't fond of reading them. In fact, they tended to avoid books. It was a minor miracle that I'd developed such a keen interest on my own.

"Now the Shield, Sophie," Lady Weatherby said. "Miss Hart, begin walking toward Sophie."

I took a few steps forward and Sophie raised her wand. "If you don't yield/I'll raise my shield."

I looked to Lady Weatherby for confirmation and she urged me forward. I stubbed my toe on an invisible wall. It was reminiscent of what happened to me at the town border.

I rubbed the tip of my foot.

"When do we use the Shield spell?" Lady Weatherby asked.

Laurel's hand rose first and Lady Weatherby nodded.

"If we are in danger and want to keep our attacker from hurting us," Laurel said.

"Couldn't all the spells be used for that?" I asked,

and quickly realized my mistake. My hand flew to cover my mouth.

"If you are under attack by a yeti, for example," Lady Weatherby began, "you would not want to use the Spasm or Blowback spells. They would not have a strong enough impact on a larger creature to allow you time to escape. Sleeping Beauty or the Shield would provide a better defense."

I raised my hand again. "Isn't there only one yeti in town?" And he owned Icebergs, the premiere place for ice cream and water ice.

The muscle in Lady Weatherby's cheek twitched. "It's simply an example."

"Okay," I said weakly.

"The Blowback spell, please, Sophie."

I was a little nervous about this one. My lower back ached on a good day. I could only guess how it would feel after a spell knocked me on my butt.

Sophie aimed her wand at me and my body stiffened. "Step on a crack/suffer blowback."

Lady Weatherby flew backward and slammed against the desk. Beakers and other glass containers scattered to the floor, breaking into pieces. Purple and green liquid oozed in the cracks in the floorboards.

Sophie covered her face with her hands, mortified. "I'm so sorry, Lady Weatherby. My wand must not have been pointed straight."

Since I'd been the one staring down the barrel of it, I could assure her the wand was perfectly straight.

Lady Weatherby regained her composure, smoothing her clothes and tucking a loose strand of black hair behind her ear. "As I said earlier, the witch's will is just as important as the wand and the incantation."

She snapped her fingers and the glass fragments reformed with the relevant liquids inside. I was desperate to know how she did that without a wand or incantations. She snapped her fingers the same way every time, yet the outcome was different. I suppose that was the type of skill level that differentiated beginners from experts.

Sophie's cheeks burned with embarrassment and she took her seat without another word.

"A wand can be dangerous in the wrong hands, Miss Hart," Lady Weatherby said. "That is why training is crucial for witches. And that is why we insist that you take your role as a witch very seriously."

"Yes, Lady Weatherby."

"Your homework is to work on these spells with your classmates. Listen and learn."

"But I don't have a wand," I objected.

"Listen and learn, Miss Hart," she repeated. "I didn't say perform the spells yourself. It's too soon."

I didn't argue. Part of me agreed with her. A wand in my incapable hand was a recipe for disaster. Sophie nearly knocked Lady Weatherby through a wall, simply because she disliked her. Her true feelings betrayed her. I understood that. I wasn't very good at hiding my emotions either.

"Witches, be sure to take Miss Hart for her owl. She'll be needing one sooner rather than later. We won't want her to miss any important announcements."

An owl? I was getting an owl?

"Class dismissed."

"Where do we go for an owl?" I asked, once we'd left school. "The forest?"

The other witches laughed.

"Paws and Claws," Millie said. "It's the animal rescue center in town."

"Right next to Petals," Laurel added.

We crossed the main road and headed to the town square. The clock tower loomed in front of us.

Paws and Claws was tucked between the flower

shop on the corner and Wands-A-Plenty. Several black cats ran to greet us when we entered.

"Do you need a familiar?" Millie asked.

"Is that what you call cats here?"

They laughed.

"No, silly," Laurel said. "You've never heard of a witch's familiar?"

I shook my head.

"Allow me to enlighten you," a man said, presumably the owner of the shop. Based on his short stature and the points of his ears, I wagered we were dealing with another elf.

"Emma, this is Chip," Sophie said. "He owns the rescue center."

"I'm an elf, in case you were wondering," Chip said with a friendly smile.

I knew he was an elf because I'd read the file in Gareth's office about the shoplifting charges against him. Seeing him in person, Chip didn't strike me as the shoplifting type. I was glad it had been a misunderstanding.

"Witch familiars are animal spirits that serve as a witch's guide or assistant in this world," Chip explained.

"Or simply as a companion," Sophie added. "My cat doesn't do any household chores."

"I gather this is all new to you," Chip said.

"It is," I agreed. "Still getting used to the idea of vampires and werewolves in my neighborhood."

"It's those harpies you should be concerned about," Chip said, and his expression soured.

"Which harpies?"

"Your neighbors." He arched a pencil thin eyebrow. "You haven't met the Minors yet? Consider yourself lucky."

"Now Chip," Begonia chastised him. "Let her decide for herself."

"Calliope's really nice," Millie added. "We play tennis together at the club."

"Stay far away from Octavia," Chip warned. "She's the grandmother. If she senses weakness, she'll eat you alive."

Laurel looked at me with solemn eyes. "No, really. She will literally eat you alive."

I swallowed hard. I'd make darn sure I kept my yard tidy and took my trashcans in straight after each collection. I didn't want to give the harpies a reason to dislike me.

"I take it you're here for an owl," Chip said.

"She is," Sophie said. "Lady Weatherby sent us."

"Then I shall put it on the coven's tab," he said. "Any type of owl in mind?"

"Take her in the back and let her see," Begonia urged.

"What will I do with an owl?" I asked.

"The owl is like your personal assistant," Chip explained. "He or she will deliver messages, run errands, and attend certain classes with you."

The four witches nodded.

"They're indispensable," Millie said.

"They keep the mice away too," Laurel added.

"How is it different from a familiar?" I asked.

Sophie's nose scrunched. "Well, because they're *owls*."

We stepped into the back room and my eyes lit up. It was as though we'd entered another building entirely. The room's ceiling was so high, I couldn't even see it. Animals were everywhere I turned. Cats, dogs, hamsters, owls, and snakes. And then there were the more unusual animals—a three-headed dog, a fish-tailed goat, and a horned animal I didn't recognize.

"You've rescued all of these?" I asked.

"Yes," Chip replied. "Some have been here since the town was cursed and their owners have passed or abandoned them. Others wander in from the forest."

"Why can't animals cross the town border?" I

asked. "They're not all supernatural."

"Oh, some can," Chip said. "It's just that the area is so remote and prone to snow in the winter, I wouldn't dream of setting them loose there. Their chances of survival would be minimal."

Several owls swooped above our heads. Chip didn't seem to believe in cages.

The elf whistled and a brown owl landed on his arm. "This is Tonto." He addressed the owl. "Tonto, this is Emma. She's in need of an owl."

The owl cocked its head and studied me with its round eyes. After a moment, he flew off.

"That's a no then," I said. Rejected by an owl. That was a new low, even for me.

"Don't worry," Laurel said. "You'll know the right owl when you see it."

"Incoming," a voice said. "Break left."

I jumped to the left and narrowly avoided being doused with bird poop. I glanced up to see a spotted owl gliding to a nearby tree branch.

"Thanks for the warning," I said.

Everyone looked at me.

"I dodged a bullet there," I said, and pointed to the poop on the ground next to me.

"We didn't warn you," Sophie said.

"I know. The owl did."

They exchanged surprised glances.

"The owl spoke to you?" Chip asked, not bothering to contain his excitement.

"Yes, that one," I said. I pointed to the sullen owl on the tree branch.

"Sedgwick," Chip whispered. "Of course." He let loose a shrill whistle. "Sedgwick, come down here."

"I'm coming," the owl said. "No need to burst anyone's eardrum."

I laughed.

"What's so funny?" Begonia asked.

"The owl is," I said. "Why can't you hear him? Isn't it a witch thing?"

"We are only able to speak to our cats," Millie explained. "The owls understand us, but we don't communicate with them telepathically."

Then why could I? I stood quietly for a moment and realized I couldn't hear all the owls. Only Sedgwick.

The spotted owl landed on Chip's outstretched arm.

"So are you going to be my new mommy?" the owl asked, his tone dripping with sarcasm.

"Um, I don't know," I said.

The owl's yellow eyes bore into mine. "What

kind of witch are you? I sense power but also…you reek of humans."

"That makes sense," I said. "Because I only found out I was a witch recently. I've lived as a human for the past twenty-five years."

"You don't need to speak out loud to me," Sedgwick said. "I can hear you just fine if you talk to me in your head."

I realized that everyone was still staring at me.

"He understands me," I said. "He said I can talk to him telepathically."

Chip offered his arm. "Would you like to hold him?"

I'd never held an owl before. He looked heavy. "How much does he weigh?"

"Hey," Sedgwick objected. "That's personal."

"About two pounds," Chip said. So not heavy at all.

"Snitch," Sedgwick snapped.

I held out my arm and Sedgwick hopped over to perch there. My arm dipped a bit at first, but then I easily kept him aloft.

"So he'll come to class with me?" I asked. I hoped he didn't cause any trouble with Lady Weatherby. Then again, she wouldn't be able to hear his caustic remarks.

"Not every day," Begonia said. "We'll let you know when."

"I feel confident that Sedgwick is your familiar," Chip said.

"But shouldn't it be a cat?" I asked. "Does anyone have an owl?"

"Not in Spellbound," Chip said. "But it's probably because your coven is different from the one here. Most of the witches trapped in this town can trace their ancestry back to the same coven."

"I don't know anything about my coven," I said.

"The fact that you have a link to owls will give you a place to start," he assured me.

"This is so cool," Laurel said. "My owl is boring."

"Yes, but Delilah is lovely," Millie said. "All of our cats are lovely."

"They are." Chip beamed with pride as though he'd made the cats himself.

I lifted the owl closer to my face. "How about it, Sedgwick?" I said. "Do you want to come and live in the most depressing house you've ever seen?"

Whatever. I don't wake up before noon and under no circumstances will I do dishes, Sedgwick said.

"You have a deal."

CHAPTER 6

THE SOUND of a church organ brought me to my feet. I was going to have to replace that doorbell. It didn't suit me at all. In fact, it made my skin crawl.

I opened the door to see two squat fairies on the front porch. One clutched a bucket and the other clutched a mop.

"Hi there," the fairy with the yellow wings said. "I'm Bernadette and this is Lila. We run Fairy No-Dust. It occurred to us that you might want a little help cleaning up your new home."

Her smile was so bright, I resisted the urge to grab my sunglasses, except, of course, that I no longer owned sunglasses. They were back in my apartment, along with the rest of my human belongings.

"You will definitely have your work cut out for

you," I said. "Parts of the house have been a bit neglected."

They clapped their hands in unison.

"Delightful," Bernadette said.

Behind them, two more fairies appeared.

"You brought reinforcements already?" I queried.

Bernadette whipped around. "Back off, Kendra. This is our turf."

The fairy presumably named Kendra landed on the porch with grace and ease. She popped a hand on her slender hip. "You don't own the northwest corner, Bernie."

Bernadette folded her arms. "We got here first."

Kendra muscled her way between them. "Hi, I'm Kendra and this is my business partner, Fiona. We own The Magic Touch. If you want this place to sparkle like a diamond, we're your fairies."

Well, I wouldn't mind the place sparkling like a diamond. I certainly wasn't capable of making that happen with my lack of upper body strength.

"How much do you charge?" I asked. "I don't have any money yet." In fact, I had no idea when or how much I got paid. It wasn't exactly a typical job offer.

"You can owe us," Bernadette said quickly. "We take IOUs from respectable citizens."

Kendra stood directly in front of Bernadette.

"You can owe us, too. A standing order. Or we'd even consider a trade of some kind."

Bernadette raised a pale eyebrow. "Like what? The next time one of you gets arrested, she'll defend you for free?"

The next time? I tried to imagine what kind of criminal mischief the fairies might be involved in.

"How about this?" I ventured. "Bernadette, your team can do downstairs and Kendra's team can do upstairs. Whichever team does the best job wins the contract."

The fairies exchanged smug looks.

"You're on," Bernadette said, more to her arch nemesis than to me.

"Name the time and place," Kendra said.

"Um, I think we know the place," I said awkwardly.

Kendra continued to try to outstare her competition without blinking. "Then just name the time."

"I need to go out," I said. "If you want to start now." I wasn't about to look a gift cleaning fairy in the mouth.

"We can do now," Bernadette said.

"So can we," Kendra replied.

"Don't let the owl out of the house and watch out

for the cat," I warned them. "He's not exactly the warm and fuzzy kind."

"Oh, cats love us," Kendra said. "Don't worry about a thing."

"Cats love us, too," Bernadette said and paused, unsure what additional evidence she could provide. "A lot. They love us a lot."

"And please don't touch Gareth's belongings," I added. "I'll take care of them another time." I wanted to go through everything and make appropriate piles, although I suspected the lion's share of items would fall into the 'donate' pile.

"We won't need to touch any of his things," Bernadette sang. "We'll simply give the place a good scrub. Clear away those nasty cobwebs on the main floor."

"Thanks," I said. "Sounds perfect. I'll be at Gareth's office if anyone needs me." It sounded like such an odd thing to say. I also wasn't sure how anyone would reach me if they needed to, since phones didn't seem to exist here.

Feeling excited by the prospect of a clean house, I grabbed a shoulder bag and began the long walk into town.

Gareth's office was remarkably neater than his house. File folders were stacked on the corner of the desk. A quill and inkpot rested in front of me. I plucked the top folder from the pile and flicked through it. The paperwork was all about Mumford's case. There wasn't much there, to be honest. One of the council members had said the evidence against Mumford was flimsy and this file seemed to support his statement.

A door opened to what I thought was a closet and a head popped through it. The head was covered with a crimson headscarf.

I screamed and nearly fell off my chair.

"Ah, there you are," a woman said. "You must be my new boss."

Not a closet then.

She entered the office and stood in front of the desk. She was tall, nearly six feet, and her cheek-bones looked as chiseled as the fountain statues.

"I'm Althea," she said, her brow creasing. "Did no one tell you about me?"

"Sorry, no," I replied, my heart still pounding. I regained my composure and smiled. "You're Gareth's assistant?"

"I was." She lowered her head and I was sure I heard the faint sound of hissing.

"What's that noise?" I asked.

Althea paused to listen. "I don't hear anything."

"It sounds like hissing."

Her face lit up. "Oh. You hear the snakes."

"Do we have an office pet?" I asked slowly.

Althea patted her headscarf. "No. They're here. I keep them covered so I don't turn you to stone. The hazards of being a Gorgon in the modern world."

I stared at her. Did my new assistant just tell me she was a Gorgon?

"You seem taken off guard," Althea said. "Don't worry. I don't bite. They do," she said, glancing upward, "but I don't let them out unless it's for self-defense. There've been a few incidents with werewolves in the pub where I had to let the girls out, you see."

"I...I've never met a Gorgon before." I didn't know what else to say. Telling her that she scared the living daylights out of me probably wasn't the best start to our professional relationship.

"There are three of us in Spellbound," she said. "I work here. My older sister, Miranda, has her own photography studio and my younger sister, Amanda, makes garden gnomes."

"Makes them?" I pictured gnomes running for

their lives as Amanda turned them to stone for the residents' garden pleasure.

"The old-fashioned way," she said, and then laughed. "I guess technically our way is the old-fashioned way, but you know what I mean."

"So how long did you work for Gareth?" I asked.

Althea sighed. "Many years. He was wonderful. A heart of gold. Not easy to find in a vampire. Trust me, I've looked."

"Were you ever...involved?" I asked.

"Goodness, no. I prefer my males with more color in their cheeks. Besides, fangs scare the girls." She pointed to her head.

A knock on the door startled me. "Am I expecting anyone?"

She bit her lip. "Oops. I meant to tell you. Mumford's here. Gotta go." She scurried back to her room as the office door opened. I'd need to ask why the front door emptied into my office instead of my assistant's. The layout didn't appear to make sense. I couldn't worry about that now, though. Not while I had a goblin standing in front of me. He wasn't at all what I expected. Not that I had expectations regarding goblins.

"You must be Mumford," I said. There was no nice way to say it—he was hard on the eyes. Lumpy, bumpy, and grumpy. His limbs were too long for his body and his face reminded me of a frog. There was no chance kissing this guy would turn him into a handsome prince.

"And you must be my new attorney." He gave me a cursory glance. "A witch, is it?"

I forced a smile. "So they tell me."

"Have you met the witches in your class?" he asked.

"I have. Everyone seems nice." Except Lady Weatherby, but I'd never utter those words aloud.

"I know a few witches from the gym," he said. "Begonia and Sophie are regulars there."

I pictured Sophie falling on the treadmill and dropping weights on her toe. It was none of my business, but the gym didn't seem like a safe place for her.

"Begonia helped me once when I got locked in the sauna," he said. "Some of the werewolves thought it would be funny to steam clean a goblin." His face grew flushed with anger. "I kept my membership, but I haven't been back since."

As unattractive as he was in general, I couldn't help but notice the state of his neck.

"Mumford, I don't mean to be rude, but your neck looks atrocious," I said.

Mumford absently touched the swollen side of his neck.

"Are you developing a goiter?" I knew nothing about goiters, but it seemed like the kind of ugly thing someone in Spellbound would have. Instinctively, I touched my own neck.

"I think it's from where Gareth tried to bite me, Miss Witch," he said.

I froze. "Gareth tried to bite you?"

He nodded mournfully.

"Did you tell anyone?" Surely someone would have mentioned it to me.

He shook his head. "Everyone's been so upset about his death, I didn't think they'd want to hear anything negative about him. They'd accuse me of acting evil again. Goblins are always accused of acting evil. I don't hear anyone accusing the dwarves of being disagreeable."

I inhaled deeply and sat on the edge of my desk. "Did Gareth often try to bite others in town?"

Mumford folded his hands in his lap. "Not that I know of, Miss Witch."

"Mumford, can you please stop calling me that?"

He gave me a blank look. "But that's your name."

"No," I said tersely. "My name is Emma Hart. You

may call me Emma or Miss Hart, whichever you're more comfortable with."

"I'm comfortable with Miss Witch."

I groaned in exasperation. "We should take you to the doctor. You need to have your neck examined. It looks like it might be infected."

"We don't really have doctors in Spellbound, Miss Wi...Miss Hart. Just healers."

I hopped off the desk. "Whatever. Let's go see the healer."

He shifted his head from side to side. "It has been sore."

"Why don't you speak up, Mumford?" I asked.

"Been distracted with the trial and then Gareth," he said. "Everything else fades away."

I understood what he meant. Since my arrival in Spellbound, I knew I wasn't firing on all cylinders.

"Come on, Mumford. I'm taking you to the healer. Someone has to look out for you if you won't do it for yourself."

Reluctantly, he got up from the chair and followed me out of the office.

"So which way?" I asked, once we were on the sidewalk.

"Left and then two blocks."

The healer was a druid by the name of Boyd.

I stood in the corner of the room while he examined Mumford's neck.

"It's an infection. That's for certain," Boyd said. I expected a druid to wear some sort of long, brown robe, but Boyd's plaid shirt and jeans were more mountain man than mystical. Maybe I was confusing a druid with a monk.

"Can you treat it?" I asked.

"I'll need to run some tests," Boyd said. "Make sure it hasn't moved to the bloodstream."

"Any idea what caused it?" I didn't ask about vampire fangs. I'd leave that to Mumford.

Boyd shrugged. "Could be any number of things. When you don't clean a wound," he said pointedly, "it increases the likelihood of infection."

"Mumford has a lot on his mind," I said. I felt sorry for the goblin.

"I hear you're defending him now," Boyd said. I watched as he wiped the swollen area with some kind of ointment and applied a bandage.

"Word travels quickly," I said.

"My assistant will be in shortly to draw blood," Boyd told Mumford.

The goblin shifted uncomfortably on the table.

"Do you not like needles, Mumford?" I asked. I

hated the pointy suckers, but Mumford was a goblin. I guess I expected him to be tougher.

"Oh, we don't use needles," Boyd said.

What was left? "You don't use leeches, do you?" If that was the case, I could understand the goblin's wariness.

"No leeches," Boyd said, a smile tugging the corners of his mouth. "It's a magic siphon. We just poke a tiny hole in the skin and the blood is sucked up into the siphon."

"I could have used a magic siphon when I was growing up," I said. Needles were on my long list of things-that-made-me-anxious.

"We'll have the results soon," he said. "In the meantime, keep using the ointment. You may feel a little lethargic today, but the effect should wear off by tomorrow."

"Thank you," I said.

"Thank you for bringing him in."

"No problem." Someone had to take care of the poor goblin. It was as though the whole town had forgotten him in the wake of Gareth's murder.

We returned to the office to talk about the case. The meeting didn't last long, though. Mumford began to droop halfway through my second question.

"Why don't we continue this when you're feeling better?" I suggested.

"Yes, I think that would be wise." Mumford staggered to the door.

"Can I call you a cab or something?" Did they have cabs in Spellbound?

He waved me off as he stumbled out of the office. "I'll be fine."

With me as his only hope for freedom, I wasn't so sure.

CHAPTER 7

SINCE I COULDN'T SLEEP, I decided to make myself useful and track down Gareth's vampire friends. I had a couple of questions to ask, including 'would anyone like a cat'? Althea had suggested that I try the Spellbound Country Club during the off hours.

It felt odd to be going to a country club in the middle of the night. Even though the vampires could be out in daylight due to the enchanted nature of the town, they still preferred to be cloaked in darkness. I didn't love the idea of walking through town at night, not with all the strange creatures afoot. I didn't have a choice, though. If I wanted to get things done, I had to leave the house. Sedgwick decided to accompany me, although he kept a reasonable distance. While I was on the hunt for vampires, he was on the hunt for dinner.

Unfortunately for my aching feet, the country club was located on the other side of town not far from the mayor's mansion. It looked as you would expect. There was a valet out front, presumably to collect brooms or other modes of supernatural transport. I was surprised when the young man greeted me by name. Another elf.

"Right this way, Miss Hart." He held open the door for me with a pleasant smile.

"Thank you," I said hesitantly. Was my picture on a wanted poster or something? It made me slightly uncomfortable that everyone in town seemed to know my name, especially when I still felt so ignorant.

I walked through the impressive lobby of the country club. Unsurprisingly, it was empty now.

I stepped up to the counter where the manager was ready and waiting to greet me.

"Miss Hart, welcome to Spellbound Country Club," he said. I couldn't tell what kind of creature he was based on his appearance. He looked like a troll, but not as ugly. I assumed it would be rude to ask.

"Thank you so much," I said.

"Are you looking to become a member? I would be happy to discuss the details with you," he said.

"Not today, thank you. I'm looking for a few

friends of Gareth's. I understand there might be a few vampires with a tee time tonight."

He looked mildly surprised. "Why, yes. They're probably around the fifth hole right now. I can have someone escort you there." He snapped his fingers and a centaur appeared behind me.

"Patrick will take you to them."

My brow lifted. Take me—as in for a ride? I studied the centaur.

The centaur smiled at me. "Climb aboard, Miss Hart. We'll be there in two shakes of a minotaur's tail."

Minotaurs shook their tails? I'd have to see that to believe it. Reluctantly, I stepped toward the centaur and he held out his hand to assist me. As he lowered his hind legs, I swung a leg over his back and nearly toppled over. With one leg hooked around his back and the other on the ground, I dangled there helplessly. The manager rushed out from behind the counter to help me look less like a fool. He had his work cut out for him.

"I'm sorry," I said. "It's my first time mounting a centaur."

Patrick stifled a laugh. "You don't say?"

"Haven't you ridden a horse?" the manager asked.

"Um, no." I'd lived a relatively sheltered life. Until now.

With the manager's help, I managed to stay atop the centaur's back.

"Good luck," the manager said. "Please do consider joining. We love diversity in our membership."

"I'll think about it," I said. Although I wasn't interested in golf, I did always want to learn how to play tennis. No time like the present.

Patrick carried me through the automatic doors at the back of the clubhouse. It was a bumpy ride. It reminded me of the hayrides I used to take at Halloween as a child. Uncomfortable, yet still mildly enjoyable.

I caught sight of Sedgwick circling above me, probably laughing his tail feathers off. Jerk.

As promised, we found the vampires on the fifth hole. There were three of them, sipping what appeared to be Bloody Marys and looking ridiculous in plaid trousers and hats with pom-poms. I was under the impression vampires were more dignified.

"Gentlemen," Patrick said, galloping to greet them. "May I present Miss Hart?"

I gave a nervous wave and attempted to slide off Patrick's back without sustaining a head injury. One of the vampires handed his drink off to another one and came over to assist me.

"Here, let me help you." His voice was smooth like silk.

"It's okay. I can do it."

Patrick's hind legs dropped to the ground and I shifted my butt to the side, preparing to hurl myself off. The vampire leaned over and whispered in my ear. "Trust me, buttercup, you don't want to fall in front of this lot. You'll never live it down."

I sat still and let the vampire lift me off in one swift movement.

"Thank you," I said.

"Shall I wait for you, Miss Hart?" Patrick asked.

The thought of getting on and off the centaur again made me queasy.

"No," the vampire said quickly. "No worries, Patrick. We'll see her safely back to the clubhouse."

"Thank you, Mr. Hunt." Patrick bowed slightly before galloping away.

I held out my hand. "Emma Hart. Nice to meet you, Mr. Hunt." I looked at him for the first time—really looked at him—and realized with a start how handsome he was. I was shaking the hand of an attractive vampire. Kill me now. Wait! Don't kill me now. Wrong expression. I hoped he couldn't read minds. Was telepathy a vampire trait or was that just in the movies?

"Miss Hart, why are you squinting at me?" he asked.

My eyes widened. "Was I? Sorry, it's so dark out here. Hard to see everyone."

The vampire holding the golf club came over to shake my hand. "A pleasure, Miss Hart. I'm Samson and this is Edgar."

The handsome vampire smiled and I noticed his fangs for the first time. They weren't as pronounced as I expected.

"Demetrius," he said.

"Hi," I managed to say. My stomach felt like butterflies in a blender. I couldn't tell which made me more nervous—the fact that I was surrounded by vampires alone in the dark or the fact that Demetrius Hunt was really, really hot.

I hedged my bets and chose fear.

"How can we help you, Emma?" Edgar asked, draining his Bloody Mary. I noticed he had a red mustache. It looked far more gruesome than a milk mustache.

"You might have heard I'm taking over Gareth's cases," I said, suddenly acutely aware that I'd stepped into their permanently dead friend's shoes in nearly every respect.

"And his house," Edgar said. "Perhaps his bank account as well?"

"Enough, Edgar," Demetrius said. "We all know Gareth's job was thankless and his house was a money pit. Spellbound isn't doing this young lady any favors."

Um, thanks?

"Well, I'm here because you're his friends and I thought you'd be able to answer some questions I have."

"Such as?" Edgar prodded.

Okay, he was going to be a pain in the butt. I could tell. I decided to start simple.

"Did Gareth have a cat?" I assumed Mr. Cat hadn't purchased his own cans of tuna, but in this town, who could be sure?

Demetrius burst out laughing. "That hairless monster is a cat? And here I thought it was some sort of ogre cursed by a miniaturization spell."

"His pantry is full of cat food," I said, "so I'm willing to go out on a limb and say it's a cat. Do you know its name?"

The vampires exchanged glances.

"Mr. Furry Face?" Edgar offered weakly.

"No, wasn't it Sunshine?" Demetrius said.

So Gareth was a fan of irony. Good to know.

Samson snapped his fingers. "Magpie. It was definitely Magpie."

What a relief. "Thank you. That's helpful. So I take it from your reactions that no one would be interested in adopting Magpie?"

My suggestion was met with stony silence.

"Anything else?" Demetrius asked.

I tried not to stare into those intense dark eyes. Maybe he was trying to glamour me. I didn't even know if that was a real vampire trick. I was going to have to hit the library sooner rather than later. Or the bookstore. Juliet was meant to be a fountain of knowledge.

"Yes, as a matter of fact there is. I met with Mumford..."

They groaned in unison.

"What's wrong with Mumford?" I asked.

"I'll write you a list," Edgar said, and raised an eyebrow. "In blood."

I could tell he was trying to get a rise out of me, so I ignored him. "He seems sweet," I said. "I feel sorry for him."

Samson patted my shoulder. "How fitting. You have Gareth's heart."

"Except hers probably beats," Edgar said.

"I believe it does," I replied. At least I hoped so. I hadn't checked since I arrived here. I resisted the urge to check my pulse. I'd wait until I was alone.

"What do you need to know about Mumford?" Demetrius prompted.

"He says that Gareth tried to bite him, and I was wondering..." I didn't get to finish my sentence. The three vampires began yelling at the same time.

"Impossible!"

"Nonsense."

"Ridiculous."

I took a step back and held up my hands. "Listen, I'm not here to accuse Gareth of anything. I just thought maybe—if it wasn't an isolated incident—then there could be a situation where he tried to bite the wrong person and it ended up in Gareth's murder."

The vein in Edgar's forehead throbbed and he came dangerously close to me. "Let's get one thing straight, shall we? Gareth was a gentle soul who would, never ever bite anyone."

Demetrius grabbed Edgar by the arm and yanked him away from me. "Enough, Edgar. Emma said she isn't here to accuse him. She only wants to help." He looked at me. "Edgar is right, though. Gareth wouldn't dream of biting anyone. It wasn't in his nature." He hesitated. "Well, I suppose it ought to have been."

"But it wasn't," Samson said. "We even made fun of him for it."

"It's why he was so suited to the role of public defender," Edgar said softly. "He cared about everyone in this town."

"You guys seem to find Mumford annoying," I said. "Is it possible that Gareth was just expressing frustration with his client? Maybe he wanted to scare him?"

Edgar folded his arms across his scrawny chest. "Not a chance."

Next topic. "Do you know anything about the petition he was preparing to file?" I asked.

Samson's brow furrowed. "What kind of petition?"

"To remove holy water from the church."

They looked surprised.

"He was planning to go ahead with that?" Demetrius asked. "We thought it was a joke."

"Do you ever attend church here?" I asked.

The three vampires howled with laughter.

"Okay, okay," I said. "I get the picture. I had to ask." I thought for a moment. "Who would object to the petition, assuming he or she was aware of it?"

Edgar scratched the stubble on his chin. "Myra is the only one I can think of."

"Who's Myra?" I asked.

"She's the church administrator," Edgar said. "But don't be fooled by her just because she's a gnome. For a lady who organizes church bingo, she has a wicked tongue."

"Who would even attend church here?" I asked. Other than Daniel, the fallen angel, I couldn't think of anyone who fit the bill.

"You'd be surprised, dear," Edgar said. "It's a social hub. Doesn't seem to matter what your origin is."

"And this is your social hub," I said, gesturing to the golf course.

Demetrius smiled. "One of a few."

I didn't ask about the others. From his wolfish expression, I had the feeling they weren't places I'd care to frequent.

"Well, thank you for taking the time to answer my questions," I said. "I appreciate it."

"Let us know if we can help with anything," Samson said. "His house is probably overwhelming for you." He hesitated. "If you decide not to keep the disco ball, send me a message and I'll take it off your hands."

"Sure."

Demetrius escorted me back to the clubhouse, where the manager offered to drive me home in one of the magic golf carts. I was relieved he didn't offer Patrick's services again.

Sedgwick followed overhead as we rode across town in the darkness. He seemed more animated than usual.

Can we do this again tomorrow night? he asked excitedly. *The golf course was full of rodents.*

Ugh. *Thanks for the tip.*

I arrived home to see the fey lanterns bursting with light.

"Who did that?" I asked Sedgwick as I walked up the porch steps.

I bet they're on a timer.

I still had so much to learn, but I was too tired to learn anything else tonight. I dragged myself upstairs and fell blissfully into a deep sleep.

Although I was groggy the next morning, I was curious to discover what the Basic Skills class entailed. Judging by the name, it seemed to be tailor-made for me since I didn't have the first clue about being a witch.

The best thing about the class so far was that Lady Weatherby would not be teaching it. Instead, an elderly man stood at the front of the class, wearing a midnight blue pointy hat and a matching cloak. The only thing missing from his wizardly appearance was a white beard. He had the sage expression down pat, though.

"I am Professor Holmes," he said. His announcement was clearly directed at me, since the other witches had been attending his class for the better part of a year.

"Emma Hart," I said.

"I've been looking forward to meeting you, Miss Hart. It isn't every day we receive a witch from the human world."

"It isn't any day," Laurel said under her breath.

"Enlighten us, Miss Hart. What can you tell us about your background? I understand you've chosen an owl as your familiar. How interesting." He peered at me over his wire-framed glasses.

"I didn't exactly choose Sedgwick," I said. "It just sort of happened."

"And yet there is a black cat living on the premises."

"Magpie? He was Gareth's cat and he isn't black. He's more...follically challenged." And in need of a personality transplant.

"And you have limited memories of your mother?" he queried.

Despite the barrage of questions, I never once felt uncomfortable. Professor Holmes had a way of making me feel at ease. I briefly wondered whether he was using some sort of spell on me.

"Nothing to suggest she was a witch," I said. My memories of her were fragmented. A fuzzy moment at a birthday party. A voice without words. When I was very small, she'd hug me to her chest and hum, and the vibrations would soothe me. That I remembered very well. And her smell. If I smelled anything remotely similar, it acted like a time machine, transporting me straight back to early childhood. I missed her so much, yet I barely knew her.

"And how did she die, if you don't mind me asking?"

"She drowned," I said. It suddenly occurred to me, sitting in the middle of the classroom, why I may have been discouraged from spending time near bodies of water. Of course, one could argue it was a self-fulfilling prophecy—that if no one taught me to swim, I'd be more likely to drown. In any case, water made me anxious and it wasn't far-fetched to think my mother's death played a role in fueling my negative feelings.

"Murder?" he asked softly.

"No," I replied, aghast. "It was ruled accidental."

He tapped the end of his wand against the table in an absent-minded gesture. "You do realize that witches cannot swim, Miss Hart."

"Like physically can't swim?"

He nodded. "Anyone who knows anything about witches knows that much."

"Spell's bells," Begonia cried. "Maybe your mother *was* murdered."

"Or maybe she didn't know she was a witch," I said. Otherwise, she would have told me. Left me a clue of some kind. At the very least, she would have confided in my father. They loved each other. She would have trusted him.

"And your father," Professor Holmes continued. "What do you know of him? I understand he was called Barron Hart."

"Yes. He was a history teacher."

"Not his profession," Professor Holmes said. "The man himself. What was he like?"

"I don't think he was a wizard, if that's what you're asking."

"It isn't. We know he wasn't one of us."

"Oh." I shrugged helplessly. "He did his best after my mother died. I remember difficult days. Days he gave up and laid on the couch." Those were the days I made us breakfast and learned how to brew coffee. I was only seven. It amazed me now, to think about what I was capable of at such a young age.

"And then he died as well," Professor Holmes said.

"Yes." I could feel the girls staring at me. I guess they hadn't been privy to the details. "It was a car accident. The roads were icy and he hit a tree." My throat tightened. I didn't often talk about the past. My grandparents didn't like to speak of it, so I'd learned to keep the memories at a safe distance.

Professor Holmes considered me. "We're glad to have you, Miss Hart. Now is there anything you'd like to ask me?"

"Like what?"

"About being a witch, of course. This is Basic Skills class, after all." He rubbed his hands together. "Owls, broomsticks, pointy black hats. You ask the question and I will endeavor to answer it."

Naturally, my mind went completely blank. "Are there any foods I should avoid? Do witches have allergies or an intolerance of any kind?"

"Ah, good question. No tomatoes."

Tomatoes? "That's it?"

"Go easy on the dairy."

I heard murmurs of assent around me.

"I love a treat at Icebergs," Laurel said, "but I can only have the small cone."

Sophie's hand flew to her stomach. "I can't have any. It makes me nauseous."

Suddenly my own experiences with milk and butter made sense. "Will I really use a cauldron?"

"Oh, indeed," he said. "We'll do a little cauldron work in this very class, in fact."

"I'm not a very good cook," I admitted. "Does that mean I'm not going to do well with a cauldron?"

"Nonsense," Professor Holmes said. "A cauldron is entirely different from a pot on a stovetop. You mustn't think of it that way."

It was nice to feel encouraged for a change. Lady Weatherby's stern expression tended to undermine any ounce of confidence I dared to feel.

"Can witches and wizards get married?" I asked. I had no idea where that question came from.

"Yes, although many choose not to."

"Why?"

He blinked. "Because we live such long lives, of course. It's difficult to think about tethering oneself to another for such an extended period of time. Almost unnatural."

"You don't think love is everlasting?" I asked.

"I didn't say that." He frowned. "Although I suppose that is the implication."

"Are you married?" I asked.

"No, no."

"Lady Weatherby?"

"Gray ghosts, no!" He chuckled. "Not to suggest she isn't a very attractive lady, of course."

"She just scares half the males of Spellbound to death," Laurel whispered.

"Only half?" Professor Holmes said, smiling.

"What about children?" I asked.

"If we didn't have children, these fine young witches wouldn't be with us now."

"Are all your fathers wizards?" I asked. "Is that how it works?"

"No," Professor Holmes said. "You only need one parent to get the gene. Witch or wizard, it matters not."

I debated whether to ask my next question. "What about mixed marriages? Say I wanted to marry a troll. Could we have children?"

"I wouldn't have thought Wayne Stone was your

type," he teased. "Nonetheless, interbreeding is possible."

Begonia nudged me gently in the ribs. "Any particular suitor in mind?"

"Just thinking ahead," I said vaguely.

"All right then. Question time is over for today. Let's get on with the lesson." He winked at me. "But we can do this at the beginning of each Basic Skills class, Miss Hart, until you begin to feel more comfortable."

"Thank you, Professor Holmes. I appreciate it."

"Not at all. We're your coven now and we look after our own, no matter what your origin is."

I wasn't convinced that everyone in the coven felt the same way, but I appreciated the sentiment.

"Now can anyone tell me the reason cauldrons are made from cast iron?"

Millie's hand shot into the air and I listened intently, trying to absorb every detail of my new life.

I walked out of class between Millie and Sophie to see Daniel lingering outside. His moody expression brightened when he saw me.

"Hello there. I was hoping I'd run into you," he said.

I could practically feel Millie and Sophie bursting with excitement next to me.

"Do you have time for a walk?" he asked.

"I do." I said goodbye to the other girls and joined Daniel on the cobblestone. "Anywhere in mind?"

"In fact, there is." We crossed the road and walked a few blocks past Trinkets, the gift store, Broomstix, and a few other places before he stopped in front of The Mad Potter.

"Would you like to go in?" he asked.

"For what?"

"I thought you'd like to choose a piece of pottery for your new house," he said. "Make it feel more like your own."

That was very sweet of him. "Yes, I would love to."

There didn't seem to be anyone actually working in the pottery store. Everywhere I turned I saw clay pots, clay bowls, and clay jugs. None of them with decoration.

"Does anyone work here?" I asked.

Daniel chuckled. "I guess this is all new to you." He folded his arms expectantly. "What's your favorite color?"

"Blue," I said. "A soft blue, though."

"What about a complementary color?"

I mulled it over. "Blue and yellow always look nice together."

Daniel rubbed his hands together. "Then blue and yellow it is." He moved closer to the nearest clay pot. "Blue and yellow, please. Something with a little style."

"No stripes," I added quickly. I wasn't a fan of stripes. Not in clothes because they made me look too wide and not on items because it reminded me of a circus tent and I hated the circus.

I watched in amazement as paintbrushes swirled around the pot, dipping in and out of pods of paint.

"It's magic," I whispered.

"Of course it is," Daniel said. "What else?"

As amazed as I was by the whole thing, part of me was still unsettled by the experience. No one seemed in control of anything. So much was left to magic. It just didn't jive with my lawyer brain.

I continued to observe the magic pottery in action. Once the paint colors had been applied, the pot danced over to the heated kiln. Five minutes later, my pot was set on a shelf to cool.

"How do we pay?" I asked Daniel.

"The potter owes me one," Daniel said.

I looked around the empty shop. "What potter?"

Daniel patted me on the shoulder. "He doesn't need to be here in order for him to exist."

I had to imagine there was quite a lot of crime in this town, considering no one was present in their shops. No wonder they needed a public defender so desperately.

"Thank you, Daniel. I really appreciate it. This pot will definitely brighten my dark space."

Daniel smiled. "Gareth was a particularly broody vampire. I think it had something to do with his job."

"You mean the job I inherited?" That didn't make me feel good.

Daniel seemed to realize his mistake. "I'm sure it will be different for you. You seem much more upbeat."

"Well, it probably helps that I'm not a vampire."

"The rest of the vampires in town are a lively bunch." He shot me a look. "Does that surprise you?"

"No, what surprises me is that I am in a town full of vampires. And trolls. And an angel just bought me a pot."

He chuckled again. "I guess it will take some getting used to."

Once the pot had cooled, we left the shop and headed toward my new office.

"How did things go with Mumford?" Daniel asked.

"He wasn't feeling well, but we're meeting again as soon as he's able. The judge is willing to extend the trial date. Althea is taking care of the paperwork. She's very good."

"He's an interesting character," Daniel said. "I do feel sorry for him, though. It's been tough on him. First being accused, and now losing his attorney right before the trial."

"Do you think Gareth's murder has anything to do with the trial?" I asked.

"What? You think the thief felt threatened by Gareth and killed him?" Daniel looked thoughtful. "I suppose it's possible. But given that we don't know who the murderer is and we have no suspects for the theft apart from Mumford, I think it will be tough to figure out."

Things that were tough to figure out never stopped me from trying. I wasn't about to change just because my environment did. Mumford needed my help, and that was what I was good at in the human world. I was never very good at helping myself, so I made it my mission to be helpful in the lives of others.

"So why don't people seem to like Mumford?"

"Because he's a goblin. I think that's one of the reasons he became a suspect. Townsfolk don't tend to like goblins for historic reasons."

"That is so racist. You can't decide someone is a suspect purely on the basis that they're a goblin." A statement I absolutely never made in the human world.

"I think it was also the gemstone found in his pocket."

Right. There was that pesky bit of hard evidence.

"To be fair, goblins are ill-tempered and known thieves. They have a long history of hoarding treasure."

"Like dragons," I said.

He laughed. "That's a good one, Emma. Everybody knows there's no such thing as dragons."

Seriously? Spellbound had a yeti but a dragon was out of the question? I smacked my forehead.

"I guess it's time I take a closer look at the file," I said, as we arrived in front of my office door. "Thank you, Daniel. For the pot. It was sweet of you."

"It was the least I can do," Daniel said. "I still feel responsible for you getting stuck here."

"Please don't blame yourself. You didn't know I'd be able to see you."

"And I certainly never expected you to try and

save me." He gave me a wistful look and my heart melted.

"Now that I'm here, at least I'll be able to make myself useful," I said. If I didn't stay busy, I would just start feeling sorry for myself. And that didn't benefit anybody, including me. "See you around, Daniel."

CHAPTER 8

AFTER READING through Gareth's case notes and talking with Althea, I decided to head over to the church and see if I could speak with Myra. If she knew about the petition Gareth was intending to file, maybe she got angry and decided to do something about it.

Up close, the church was stunning.

I'd always been interested in architecture in a superficial sense. There'd been a pretty church in the town where I grew up. Although my grandparents weren't devout, we attended mass on special occasions like Easter and Christmas. I loved seeing the church decorated for Christmas with its display of candles and wreaths. I remembered asking them once if my mother's parents had been Christian, and

Gran had nearly bitten my head off. I never asked again.

The Spellbound church was Romanesque, made of gray stone with rounded arches and one large tower.

I passed through the entryway and the interior took my breath away. Angels carved from stone. Arched stained glass windows depicting stories from the Bible. Hand carved wooden pews. Religious or not, who wouldn't want to spend time in here?

I took my time walking down the aisle, trying to capture every detail in my mind. Weddings here had to be nothing short of magnificent. For a brief moment, I indulged in the fantasy that I was a bride walking down the aisle to my beloved. I hadn't been the type of little girl who dreamed of a fancy wedding, but I was willing to cater to my inner princess every once in a blue moon.

I was just hitting my stride when a small voice called out to me—

"Can I help you?"

I stopped, mid-wedding march and whirled around. A short, stout woman with a round face stood behind me.

"Hello," I said, slightly embarrassed. "I'm looking for Myra."

"You found her," she said. Her white hair was thick and wavy and she wore a plain green dress with black, buckled loafers. Even without the conical hat, Myra was clearly a gnome.

"I'm Emma Hart," I said, and my voice echoed in the empty church.

Myra quickly shushed me. "This is a place of worship. Not a playhouse."

I cleared my throat and spoke in a lower tone. "I'd like to ask you a few questions about Gareth in private."

"Follow me." She walked to the altar and took a left turn to a wooden stall. She opened the door and gestured for me to go inside.

"But this is a confessional," I objected. "I just want to talk to you about Gareth."

"It's the most private place in the church," Myra said.

I relented, stepping inside and closing the door behind me. I sat on the bench and waited. Two seconds later, Myra appeared opposite me, yanking open the dark curtain to peer at me. Due to her short stature, I could only see her eyes and the top of her white head.

"So I wanted to know..." I began, but Myra shushed me again.

"That's not how the confessional works."

"How would you know how a confessional works?" I shot back. "You don't even have a real priest here." Or maybe they did. Otherwise, how would they bless the water to make it holy?

Myra's wrinkled brow wrinkled even more. "Have you come to ask me questions or not?"

I was beginning to understand why Gareth hadn't filed the petition yet. "Yes, but..."

"Then you need to say, 'bless me, Myra, for I have sinned.'"

"But I haven't..."

"Come now, dear. You've been living as a human in the prime of her youth. Sinning is to be expected."

I studied the top of her head. "You can't send people to hell, can you?" I was fairly certain gnomes didn't have the power of damnation.

One white eyebrow lifted. "Why do you ask? Is there something you've done that might necessitate a visit downstairs?"

I reviewed a mental list of my imperfect behavior. "I'm already planning to get rid of Gareth's cat, even though the house is huge and we can easily co-exist."

"No problem there. Cats are horrid creatures."

"I don't know about the horrid part, but I couldn't live with one."

"I couldn't live without Bacardi," she said.

"Oh, that's so sweet. Is Bacardi your dog?"

She gave me a look of utter disdain. "No, dear, the rum."

They had Bacardi in Spellbound? "How can you have human-made rum here?"

"Oops." Myra chuckled. "I think I'm confused. You're the one meant to be confessing."

I thought more about my past transgressions. "When I was nine, I stole a handful of change from my grandfather's swear jar." I'd wanted to buy candy at the store because I was never allowed to have any at home. Gran was forever worrying about the state of my teeth.

"Change, you say?" Myra asked. "Is that a lot of money in human terms?"

"Not really," I said. "But it wasn't mine and I took it." And I never told anyone until now.

"Anything else?" Myra sounded unimpressed.

I took a deep breath. "When I was sixteen, I really, really liked my best friend's boyfriend." I'd gone to bed every night, praying they'd break up. I'd even wished for a huge zit on her chin to put him off.

"And?" Myra prompted.

"And what?"

"Did you try to seduce him?"

"No, of course not."

"Did you dress provocatively in the hopes of gaining his affection?" She stooped over the ledge and peered at my chest. "I see the potential for cleavage is there."

I laid a hand over my chest. "No, but I used to wear makeup when I knew I'd be seeing him." I tended to look like a ghost without lipstick.

She sat back down. "Did you at least kiss him?"

My shoulders sagged. "No, nothing ever happened, but that's not the point. I coveted him. Coveting is against the rules, isn't it?" I'd need to brush up on my commandments if I intended to swing by this beautiful church now and again.

"I suppose," she huffed. "This confession is incredibly lame, I'll have you know. You should hear the filth in this town. You'll never fit in."

I struggled to come up with something worse, but I couldn't. "Why do you need to hear confession anyway? You have no real authority."

"Because that's how it works."

"You're just a nosy, old cow!" I exclaimed. "You

probably use this confessional to collect information about the other residents."

"I am a gnome, not a cow," she said simply. "And your confession is putting me to sleep. Tell me why you're here so I can move onto something more interesting. Like a nap."

"I found a draft of a petition in Gareth's home office. He was planning to lodge a protest against the holy water used in the church. Did you know about that?"

She hesitated. "I knew he objected to it. He told me as much when I ran into him at the Enchanted Garden."

"What's that?"

"My husband Frank's garden center. Gareth was looking at azaleas, but he couldn't decide which kind he wanted. He mentioned that he'd like the vampires to be able to enjoy the church social scene as much as everyone else in town, but that they considered the holy water a health and safety issue."

"Did he ask you to stop using it?"

"He did."

"And what did you say?" Given the petition, I was fairly certain I already knew the answer.

"I told him to strap on his big boy fangs and get on with life."

"In those exact words?"

She paused. "No. I told him it simply isn't possible to please everybody all the time, so why bother trying?"

The more I learned about Gareth, the more I liked him. "But his request wasn't about pleasing everyone. It was about making a community space accessible to everyone."

Myra blew a raspberry. "Poppycock. Spellbound is a big town. The vamps have plenty of places to congregate. Gareth didn't need to get his fangs out of joint just because I want to keep the church sacred."

"Do you let witches come here?"

"I let you in, didn't I?"

"What about werewolves?"

"Of course. They contribute the best dishes to the potluck dinners."

Whether she was willing to admit it or not, Myra had a bias against vampires. "What did you plan to do if he filed the petition?"

She leaned her arms on the ledge of the confessional, revealing her whole face. "Gareth was the public defender. He pissed off every judge in town at one time or another."

"So you didn't see the petition as a threat?"

She laughed and plopped down on the bench. “Not even remotely.”

No motive for Myra then. “Thank you for your time.”

“We host bingo every Wednesday night if you’re interested. I’ll add you to the mailing list. My owl sends calendar updates every Monday morning.”

“Okay, sure.” Maybe if I spent enough time at the church, I’d be able to convince the other members of the community to ditch the holy water. A gesture in Gareth’s memory.

“If you’re looking for reasons someone murdered the vampire, you might want to drop in on your neighbors.”

“The harpies?”

“The Minors are a bunch of screeching shrews. Gareth was risking life and limb by complaining about the calendar. I don’t know why Sheriff Hugo hasn’t arrested the whole family.”

“What’s the calendar?”

Myra groaned. “Every year, Miss Thumb-In-Every-Honey-Pot puts together a calendar featuring the hottest males in Spellbound as a fundraiser. This year she refused to allow the vampires to show their fangs. It was too erotic or something.” She laughed and slapped her knee. "As if there was any such thing. Too erotic? Can you imagine?"

Abruptly, Myra pulled the curtain closed between us. I guess that was my cue to leave.

"Nice meeting you," I said, as I exited the confessional and immediately looked around the church in fear. What was the penalty for lying in church?

I hurried out the front door before I could find out.

On my way back into town from the church, Sedgwick intercepted me.

You're wanted in town.

"Shouldn't you have a note in your beak or something?" I asked.

They gave me one, but I dropped it. Who needs a note when I can just tell you the message?

I sighed. "What's the message?"

You are to meet Sophie and Begonia at Wands-A-Plenty.

"Really?"

Would I make this stuff up?

I hurried the rest of the way into town. Sure enough, Sophie and Begonia were waiting outside of the wand shop. I was pretty sure they were more excited than I was.

"Be sure to get a wand with a leather grip," Begonia said. "They're more expensive but well worth it."

"Doesn't the wand need to choose me?" I asked.

Sophie and Begonia cackled hysterically.

"Where did you get a silly idea like that?" Begonia asked. "We're not shopping for a unicorn."

Wait. There were unicorns here? Be still my heart.

We entered the wand shop and the inside was exactly as the name suggested. Rows and rows of wands and nothing else.

"He'll need to measure your wingspan," Sophie said. "Once we know your size, we can shop in the appropriate section."

An older gentleman with gray hair and round glasses emerged from a back room. "Why, hello. If it isn't the new witch. What a thrilling development for Spellbound."

"This is Alaric, the owner," Sophie said. "He's a wizard."

"Nice to meet you, Alaric."

"Hold out your arms, please, Miss Hart," he said from behind the counter.

He was going to measure me from there?

I extended my arms and watched as a measuring tape unrolled in front of me and extended from my left fingertips to my right. It floated over to Alaric who noted the numbers.

"A size six. Just as I suspected," he said.

"That's my size, too," Begonia said. "I know where to take you."

We disappeared down one of the long aisles and I noticed a large number six hovering in mid-air above a shelf. There were too many wands to choose from in every color imaginable.

"Grab anything you like and you can try it out," Sophie said.

"How can I try them out?" I asked. "That doesn't seem safe." Certainly not when I was at the helm.

"There's a safe zone, like a dressing area," Begonia said.

I chose half a dozen wands to take to the safe zone. It was a room behind a set of green curtains where I could practice with each wand and get a better feel for them.

Sophie and Begonia served as my assistants, teeing up the next wand and handing it to me.

"Ooh, I like that one," Begonia said, cooing over the wand in my hand. It was a pretty celadon color with a beige leather grip. "If you don't care for it, I may put it on my birthday list."

"You should get one with a different colored grip, Sophie," I said. "Then you'll remember which way to point it."

"I'm not allowed another wand until I outgrow this one," Sophie replied.

"This wand was her sister's," Begonia explained. "Except for her first wand, all the others have been hand-me-downs."

I pointed the wand at the dummy on the far side of the room. There were brown tufts of hair popping out of the dummy in all directions.

"I take it the wizard isn't a fan of werewolves," I said.

"They've trampled his roses one too many times," Sophie explained. "That's why there's an ordinance now about when and where werewolves can turn."

"This wand feels a little heavy for me," I said. "Next one, please."

Sophie handed me a Tiffany blue wand with a silver grip. "This is beautiful. It has to be too expensive for me."

"Never mind the price," Begonia said. "The coven is paying. They always pay for first wands. It's a rite of passage."

I held the wand between my fingers and examined it from end to end. "I honestly don't think I've ever owned anything as nice as this." I hadn't made a lot of money as a public interest lawyer. In fact, I was still paying off my law school loans. I wondered what would happen to my debt now. My credit would be ruined if I ever managed to leave Spellbound.

I took aim at the dummy and focused my will. "Step on a crack/suffer blowback."

The dummy blew backward and smashed against the wall. Sophie and Begonia gasped in unison.

"That's definitely your wand," Sophie said, her eyes bright. "That was better than I've managed to do all term."

I stared at the tip of the wand. My palms were sweating so much I was afraid I might drop the wand.

"I felt the energy," I said. It was like a power surge.

"I'll bet," Begonia said, and began gathering up the other wands. "Let's get this one locked and loaded. I'm starving."

I took the wand to the counter. Alaric grinned when he saw my choice.

"You have exquisite taste, Miss Hart," he said. "This one's a beauty."

"Thank you. It felt right in my hand, you know?" It truly did. Like it belonged there.

"I understand completely." He rang up the purchase. "I'll put it on the coven's tab."

"Thank you."

"You'll need to register your wand with the registrar," Alaric continued, wrapping my wand in tissue paper and placing it in a decorative case.

"Same with brooms," Sophie added. "You'll need a license, too."

"You have as much red tape here as we do," I said.

"When you're all trapped under one invisible roof," Alaric began, "rules and regulations become an absolute necessity for a civilized society." He handed me a bag with the Wands-A-Plenty logo on the side. "Good luck with it, Miss Hart."

"Thank you very much. I'll need it."

"With aim like yours," Sophie said, "don't be so sure. We should practice spells now."

"Can we practice after we eat?" Begonia asked. "I can't cast anything on an empty stomach."

"Can't seem to cast anything on a full stomach either," Sophie teased.

Begonia stuck out her tongue.

"I wouldn't mind a coffee," I said. I needed the boost. "Can we go to Brew-Ha-Ha?"

"I never turn down a peppermint twist latte," Begonia said.

The march began at sundown, just as we arrived in front of Brew-Ha-Ha.

Begonia's hand flew to cover her mouth. "This must be Gareth's funeral procession."

We stood against the wall of the building and watched as a line of vampires passed by, each one dressed in a flowing red cloak. Leading the procession was Lord Gilder, but I recognized Samson, Edgar, and Demetrius at the front. With his chiseled features and perfectly sculpted body, it was hard to miss Demetrius.

"Why red?" I whispered.

"It's their color of mourning," Sophie replied.

Demetrius caught sight of me admiring him and winked.

Begonia gripped my arm. "Spell's bells! Demetrius Hunt winked at you."

Sophie rolled her eyes. "Begonia has a thing for Demetrius."

"It's not a thing," Begonia said hotly, but I noticed

she couldn't take her eyes off the sexy vampire.

"I can certainly understand the interest," I said. "He's damned attractive." Emphasis on damned.

The line of vampires continued, with the coffin bringing up the rear. There were no pallbearers. The coffin seemed to be sustained in the air by magic.

"Is the funeral typically this long after a vampire's death?" I asked. In the human world, different religions had their own customs regarding when and how to bury the dead, so I guess it didn't surprise me.

"Lord Gilder has his own way of doing things," Sophie whispered, as though afraid to be overheard. "A coven funeral would be completely different."

"And a werewolf funeral…" Begonia let loose a low whistle. "Let me tell you—that's a party you want to attend."

I returned my attention to the long procession. "Where are they going now?"

"To the cemetery," Sophie said. "Then they'll go back to Underkoffler's for the rest of the night to eat and drink."

"What's Underkoffler's?" It didn't sound like the name of a pub.

"Piotr Underkoffler's funeral home," Begonia said.

Sophie cringed. "Ugh. Don't even say his name." She leaned over to me. "Best to avoid him if you can."

"Believe me. I have every intention of avoiding the town undertaker." I watched the back end of the casket as it disappeared from view. "Is it vampires only?"

"The procession is," Begonia said. "The party at Underkoffler's will be open to anyone." Her gaze flitted absently to the place on the cobblestone where we'd first spotted Demetrius. "Maybe we should go."

"I feel like I should out of respect for Gareth, but I can't," I said. "I have to prepare Mumford's case for trial in less than a week. That's what Gareth would have wanted."

Begonia chewed her lip, debating. "It's probably not a good idea to hang out with a room full of drunk vampires anyway."

"The ones I met seem really nice," I said. Of course, you ply enough alcohol into anyone and he can become a complete monster.

"We'll have to take you to the Spotted Owl one night," Sophie said. "It's owned by the hottest guy in Spellbound."

Begonia clutched her chest. "An incubus. His brother owns the Horned Owl. They're both divine."

"No, Daniel is divine," Sophie said. "The incubi brothers are panty melters."

"True," Begonia agreed. "But Emma already knows how divine Daniel is, don't you?" She hip checked me.

"He is definitely..." I didn't know how I wanted to describe him. "Not what I expected an angel to be like."

With the procession finished, Begonia pulled me inside the coffee shop. We ordered three lattes, mine with an anti-anxiety boost.

"You know why Daniel's fallen, right?" Sophie asked in a hushed tone.

"Not exactly." We took a table by the window. The place was practically empty, probably due to the late hour. Most people were having cocktails now instead of coffee. My body, as always, cried out for caffeine.

Begonia leaned across the table. "He liked earthly pleasures too much. Refused to give up his vices."

"Did he have anything to do with the town's curse?" I asked, remembering Juliet's version of events.

"Depends on who you ask," Sophie said. "Some

say he made the enchantress fall in love with him and then left her high and dry for his next conquest."

I hated to ask my next question, but I needed to know. "Is he still like that?"

"I know there was some scandal with Mayor Knightsbridge's daughter a while back," Sophie said.

Begonia slapped the table excitedly. "And there was a witch in our coven."

"Ginger's older sister, Meg."

Begonia pressed her lips together. "That didn't end well. Meg tried to curse him twenty ways to Sunday, but nothing worked. She was furious. I think she still is."

I thought about our trip to the pottery place and wondered how much of that was part of his ruse. Was he trying to lure me in?

"He seems so sweet," I said, taking a careful sip of my latte. I had a habit of scalding my tongue in the human world and tried not to make the same mistake here.

"He's very convincing," Sophie said. "How do you think he manages to attract so many intelligent females in Spellbound? They all know better, yet they've fallen for him anyway."

"And what about Demetrius?" I asked. "Is he a player, too?"

Begonia sighed. "I'll play any game he wants."

"What's stopping you?" I asked. "It's not like he's going to meet anyone from out of town."

Begonia smiled. "Except you."

Sophie sucked the foam off the top of her latte. "Don't let Begonia's dreamy expression fool you. Her list of potential conquests in town is longer than Santa's naughty list."

"And how many on the list have you checked off so far?" I asked.

Begonia stared into her enormous mug. "None," she mumbled.

"None?" I repeated, dumbfounded.

Begonia's pretty features twisted in a grimace. "What if I make a bad choice? We can't escape a lapse in judgment here. Everyone in town will know and live long enough to never let you forget."

Despite the anti-anxiety boost, I felt my own anxiety creeping up on me. "So if I screw up Mumford's case, no one in town will let me forget it?" Ever?

Sophie gave me a comforting pat on the hand. "Don't worry, Emma. You're going to do well. The only one who thinks Mumford is guilty is Sheriff Hugo and that's only because he caught him with the diamond."

"Sheriff Hugo thinks we're all guilty of horrible crimes that we simply haven't committed yet," Begonia complained. "He blames everyone equally for the curse."

"Even those of us who weren't born when the curse happened," Sophie added.

"It's a shame he can't see past the curse," I said. "I've met so many nice residents already." My conversation with Myra came flooding back to me. "Do you know anything about my neighbors?"

"The Minors?" Sophie asked, and I nodded.

"Why do you want to know about them?" Begonia asked.

"I need to talk to them about Gareth," I said. "And people seem to think they're bad news."

Begonia swirled the remaining liquid around in her mug. "Not bad news exactly. Just a thorn in the side of the community. The grandmother is a real pill."

"Don't get on her bad side," Sophie warned. "And if you go, bring your wand."

Was there anyone's bad side it was safe to get on in Spellbound? Probably not.

"I'm going to see them in the morning before I meet with Mumford. I call it ripping the Band-Aid.

The thing I want to do least in the day is the thing I do first."

"That's very disciplined of you," Begonia said. "I'm the opposite. I put unpleasant tasks off until the absolute last second."

"Good luck," Sophie said uneasily. "Bring Sedgwick with you for support."

"Maybe." Definitely not. Sedgwick's acid tongue was sure to make things worse rather than better.

"Rip that Band-Aid," Begonia said enthusiastically, even though she had no clue what a Band-Aid was.

I was prepared to rip it off bright and early tomorrow. I just hoped I didn't draw blood.

CHAPTER 9

THE FIRST THING I noticed about the harpies' house was the widow's walk at the top. I'd never seen a house with a widow's walk that wasn't within view of the sea. Otherwise, what was the point?

Hesitantly, I walked up the steps to the front porch. There was a huge brass knocker on the door in the shape of a bird with breasts. I gripped it awkwardly and banged away.

The door opened and my body tensed. The only thing I knew about harpies was what I had read as a child. They were hideous bird women that carried evildoers off to Tartarus. As far as I was concerned, I'd already been carried off to Spellbound and I wasn't looking to be in transit again anytime soon.

"You must be Emma." The woman who answered the door looked to be about thirty-five years old and she wasn't remotely hideous. In fact, she was downright beautiful.

"Yes, I am. I've moved in to Gareth's old house next door." Emphasis on old.

"Welcome to the neighborhood. I'm Calliope. Would you like to come in?"

"That would be nice. Thank you."

She opened the door wider and stepped back to allow me passage. The inside of the house was stuffed to the gills with *things*. Everywhere I looked there seem to be knickknacks. Decorative plates lined the walls. Dolls with button eyes and vacant expressions stared at me from shelves above. It reminded me of every old person's house I'd ever been in combined.

"This way," Calliope said. "We were just about to sit down for tea in the sunroom. Would you care to join us?"

"Yes, please."

Tea was an understatement. I stepped into the sunroom to see a large round table piled with finger sandwiches and cookies. A silver pot of tea sat on a tray with several teacups ready and waiting. There were five other women seated in the room, each one beautiful in her own way. Even the eldest, as wrinkled as she was, exuded a strange kind of beauty. It was hard to imagine these women as hideous birds.

Birds.

The presence of the widow's walk began to make more sense to me.

"Well, look what Gareth's repulsive cat dragged in," the eldest woman said.

Warmth spread to my cheeks. "I'm afraid Magpie didn't bring me here," I said. And I took offense to being called repulsive on his behalf.

"It's an expression," the older woman snapped. "I didn't intend for you to take it literally."

"I think you're just meant to say 'look what the cat dragged in.' When you add 'Gareth's' and 'repulsive' to it, it changes the meaning."

The five women stared at me. That was apparently the wrong thing to say.

The eldest woman pressed her pruned lips together. "So what brings you here besides a desire to be the smartest person in the room?"

Calliope shot a death glare at the old woman. "Grandmother, please. Why don't we make Emma feel more comfortable? She is our new neighbor, after all."

Another woman stood and moved toward the teapot. "Would you like a cup of tea, Emma?" She stopped and turned to face me. "We've been terribly rude. We should introduce ourselves, especially since we all know who you are."

Calliope pointed to the woman at the teapot. "This is my mother, Marisol. And that's my grandmother, Octavia. My Aunt Phoebe isn't here at the moment."

"Pissing away money at the Shamrock Casino again," Octavia muttered.

"Nice to meet you," I said, ignoring the remark.

"And the other two are my sisters, Darcy and Freya," Calliope continued. "I'm the middle child."

Darcy bristled. "Why do you always feel the need to say that?"

Calliope rolled her eyes. "Because it's true."

Darcy ground her teeth. "You're just trying to rub in the fact that I'm older than you.

"I think it's obvious without me mentioning it," Calliope said. I saw the hint of a smile on her lips.

Marisol poured me a cup of tea. "Milk and sugar?"

"Yes to both, please."

Marisol studied me. "How much sugar?"

The way she was looking at me, I got the sense that this was a test. How much sugar would be acceptable here? One teaspoon? Two? I didn't want to make a mistake during my very first visit. Heaven knew I'd made enough of those in Spellbound already.

"Just one, please."

Marisol smiled and I sighed inwardly with relief. One seemed to be the right answer.

She handed me the cup of tea and Calliope offered me a plate of cookies.

"They're all homemade," Calliope said. "We love to bake in this house."

"Thank you," I said. The cookies looked delicious. I didn't recognize a single type, but that didn't stop me from selecting two. I was afraid of a lot of things, but unfamiliar cookies weren't one of them.

"The reason I'm here is to ask about the calendar," I said. "Myra over at the church mentioned that you create a calendar as a fundraiser."

Darcy perked up. "That's me. Are you interested in helping? Because I can always use another set of hands." She looked around the room pointedly. "It seems I do everything around here."

I felt like I was stepping into a minefield. I nibbled on a cookie to give myself strength. "Actually, I came to ask about your disagreement with Gareth."

Darcy's eyes glittered with suppressed anger.

"Disagreement? Is Myra spreading lies about me again? That meddling gnome is unbelievable."

"No, no." I had no intention of fanning the flames of another dispute. "I went to speak to her about her own disagreement with Gareth, and she mentioned that he was unhappy with the way the calendar was being handled this year. I thought I would come and get your side of the situation."

Darcy stood and approached me at the table. "Of course. Every year I organize this calendar as a fundraiser. We include all types of men, as long as they're easy on the eyes."

From her position in the easy chair, Octavia snorted. "And just plain easy."

Darcy glared at her grandmother. "Last year, a few residents complained. The healthy display of fur and fangs put off a certain segment of buyers."

"The frigid ones," Octavia said.

"This year I decided to airbrush them out."

"Fur and fangs are a problem here?" I couldn't imagine how, given the nature of the town.

Octavia slapped her knee. "Apparently a little fur and fangs are too much for some in this town to handle. Got them all riled up. I suppose they were worried they might get humped by a werewolf on their way to the market."

"Grandmother!" the three younger harpies yelled in unison.

"So Gareth was upset about vampires' fangs being airbrushed out?" I asked.

"Yes," Darcy replied. "We generally had a good relationship, and I think he expected me to change it back when he asked." She tipped up her chin. "But I refused. After all, it's *my* project."

"Maybe if you spent less time on all these projects," Octavia said, "you'd have more time to land one of the men in your calendar. I have no intention of living with the lot of you for eternity."

"I can think of several ways to solve that problem," Darcy snapped.

"So Gareth was the angry one?" I asked, trying to stay on topic. Myra had made it sound as though Darcy was the injured party. Although she seemed a little bitchy, she didn't actually seem angry about the calendar. And why should she be? She didn't have to change anything.

"It wasn't just Gareth," she said. "There were a few objections lodged against the calendar. To be honest, sales are down so far compared with this time last year."

"Because sex sells," Octavia said. "Everybody knows that."

"Even in the human world," I agreed.

"She kept the untouched pictures for us to enjoy," Freya said. "You should see Mr. October with that strategically placed ear of corn." She ran her tongue over her top lip. "Yummy."

"You should go out with him," Octavia urged. "Then one of you might actually get out of this house."

"He's a werewolf," Marisol said. "The only place Freya would be going with him is…"

Darcy covered her ears. "Thank you for your contribution, Mother."

"It's too bad Daniel refused to participate again," Calliope said. "You'd probably have to do another print run."

"Oh, please," Octavia said. "Half the females in this town have seen him naked."

"Yes, but that was ages ago," Calliope reminded her.

"Daniel Starr?" I asked. "The angel?"

"*Fallen* angel," Darcy corrected me. She looked me up and down. "That's right. He's the reason you're here, isn't he?"

I shrank back. "Not like that. I thought I was helping him…" I hesitated, unwilling to tell them more. Not this gossipy bunch. "It was just a big misunderstanding."

"I'd love to have a big misunderstanding with Daniel. He's dreamy," Freya said. "If he came calling, I'd happily leave this house."

"Then let's make it happen," Octavia said. "I'd even offer a dowry."

"Grandmother, no one has dowries anymore," Calliope said.

"I guess that explains why I have a house full of harpies," she griped.

"Speaking of misunderstandings," Darcy said, snapping her fingers. "I heard that Gareth had a huge argument with his former fiancée in the middle of the bookstore."

Freya's eyes grew round. "That's right. Pandora told me all about it when I ran into her at the salon a couple of weeks ago."

"Gareth was engaged?" I asked. That was the first time anyone had mentioned a fiancée. Not even Althea had mentioned her.

Darcy gave a dismissive wave. "They ended it last year. It was some kind of power play that did them in. She didn't want to move into his house and he refused to move into hers."

"What was the fight in the bookstore about?" I asked.

"No clue," Darcy replied. "You'll have to ask Alison. She's usually in her music studio downtown."

"Lovely singing voice," Octavia said. "Too bad none of you can carry a tune."

"We're not sirens like her," Calliope said. "We end up sounding like screeching birds."

"Like fingernails on a cauldron," Octavia agreed.

I set down my teacup and thanked them. "I'm sorry to have come here with so many questions on my first visit. It's just that I've been spending so much time in Gareth's house and his office, I feel like I owe it to him to solve his murder."

"You're already doing more than that lazy, good-for-nothing centaur," Octavia said. "Maybe you should take over his job, too."

"Grandmother, Sheriff Hugo is excellent," Calliope said. "It's not easy being the sheriff in a town of supernaturals."

"Says you," Octavia sniffed.

"Well, it was great to meet you all. Thanks for the tea and cookies."

"Come by anytime," Calliope said and smiled warmly.

"Yes, it's always nice to have fresh meat," Octavia said.

My stomach knotted as I headed toward the front door. I really hoped that was a Spellbound idiom. With Octavia Minor, it was hard to tell.

After a productive meeting with Mumford at the office, I decided to follow up on the tip from the harpies regarding Gareth's former fiancée.

Alison's studio wasn't hard to find. It was on a quiet side street behind the town square on the second floor of the building. She was finishing up with a student when I arrived. I sat on the folding chair outside the room and listened to the end of the lesson.

Her voice was spine-tinglingly amazing. Listening to her hit those high notes, I could easily imagine sailors plunging to their watery deaths in an effort to reach the source of that incredible sound. I'd noticed a piano in one of Gareth's living rooms. He must have been a fan of music, too.

The singing stopped and I heard the student ask a question about the next lesson. A moment later, a young elf appeared in the waiting area. She looked no older than ten, with the trademark pointy ears and adorable blond pigtails.

"Hello," she said, eyeing me suspiciously. "I don't recognize you. Are you here for singing lessons?"

"No," I said honestly. "I'm here to speak to Alison."

"I'm Alison." Her throaty voice took me by surprise. After hearing her sing, I was expecting someone with higher pitch.

"Hi Alison. I'm..."

"I know who you are," she said abruptly. She shooed the elf out the door. "Make sure you practice. Don't come next week with the same breathing mistakes or I'll drown you in a bucket of lemon fizz."

My eyes widened until the young elf burst into laughter. "You're so funny, Alison."

Alison broke into a smile and held the door open for the elf. "Say hi to your mom and dad."

"I will."

Alison turned to me. "So you're living in Gareth's house and you've taken over his job. Let me guess. You're here to ask for my hand in marriage to make it a clean sweep."

"Not exactly," I said.

She walked into her studio and I hurried after her.

"Did you find something of mine in his house?" she asked. "I never did find my favorite pink cardigan. He swore up and down he didn't have it."

"If I come across it, I'll let you know." I cleared my throat. She seemed nice, but intimidating—a more agreeable combination than Octavia who was both disagreeable and scared the crap out of me.

Alison folded her arms and stared at me. "So why are you here?"

"Wouldn't you like to know who's responsible for the murder of your former fiancé?" I asked.

"The sheriff said he'd tell me when he knew something." Alison arched an eyebrow. "Do *you* know something?" I couldn't tell whether she was interested because she was the culprit or because she cared.

"Not yet," I said. "I'd heard about a fight between the two of you and wanted to ask you about it."

She laughed—a deep, throaty laugh that would have suggested cigarette smoking if that had existed in Spellbound. "Which day of the week?"

"You fought a lot?"

She crossed the room and began tidying up music books. "Why do you think we ended our engagement?"

"I was told it was because you each refused to move into the other's house."

Alison smiled gently. "That was part of it, sure. The other part was that we fought all the time. Fighting with someone day in and day out is exhausting, especially when you're immortal." She sighed and stared into space. "Eternity seems mighty long when you're tied to the wrong person."

"Did you love him?" I asked.

She rounded on me. "Of course I loved him! He was the kindest, most intelligent..." She stopped, struggling not to cry. "Gareth was wonderful and I still miss him, but I know we made the right call."

"Has he dated anyone else since you ended your engagement?" I asked.

"Not that I know of," she said.

"So the fight in the bookstore," I prompted. "Do you remember what that was about?"

Alison shrugged. "No idea. If I had to guess, I would say it was over the books. We had different taste in reading material, you see. He preferred gothic romance and I like epic adventures with a lot of death and destruction."

Go figure.

"Thanks for your time," I said. "If I find anything

of yours, I'll be sure to pass it along." I made a move for the door when she spoke again.

"So what's your take on Mumford?" she asked.

I stopped and turned to face her. "What about him?"

"Do you think he's guilty of stealing those jewels?"

Guilty? Did anyone in town think Mumford was guilty other than the sheriff? "I can't really discuss it. Confidentiality and all."

"Gareth used to say that, too," she said wistfully. "He seemed to have changed his tune about Mumford, though."

"What makes you say that?" I didn't see anything in the files that suggested Gareth disbelieved him.

"Nothing specific," she replied. "It's just that he'd been anxious to get the trial over and done with so Mumford could get back to his life. Then suddenly, he seemed to be trying to slow things down. I ran into him at the Enchanted Garden not long before he died." She paused, remembering. "He was looking at azaleas and I bought a tomato plant. Anyway, he seemed upset so I asked him about it. He'd apparently argued with Mumford earlier that day. Whatever they discussed was still bothering him."

"He didn't tell you what it was?"

"No, and I didn't ask. I was always a little bent out of shape when I ran into Gareth unexpectedly. Part of me wanted to drag him home with me and the other part of me wanted to kick him in the shins and run away."

She sounded so conflicted. My heart ached for her.

"Thanks for the information," I said. No one else had mentioned an argument between Mumford and Gareth. Maybe it had something to do with the bite on Mumford's neck.

"If I remember anything more, I'll contact you," she said.

"I'm sorry for your loss, Alison," I said, and left.

CHAPTER 10

I WAS RELIEVED to be dealing with beakers instead of wands today. My wandwork wasn't faring too well, so I embraced the possibility that potions would eventually be my true calling.

I sat between Laurel and Millie, as Ginger lectured us about the different types of potions.

"There are many more advanced potions, of course, but you won't be introduced to those anytime soon." Ginger stepped away from the desk and stood in front of the long table.

"What kind of advanced potions?" I asked. I liked that Ginger didn't seem to mind my constant questions or failure to raise my hand. She was much more laid back than Lady Weatherby.

Ginger ticked off each one on a finger. "Death potions, clone potions, love potions..."

"Really?" I queried. "Love potions actually work?"

"It's fairly complicated and there are other factors to consider, but yes," Ginger replied. She rested her elbows on the table and smiled at me. "But from what I understand, you won't be needing any help in that department, honey."

"Demetrius Hunt winked at her," Begonia complained. "Can you believe it? I've been dying for him to notice me."

"Maybe that's your problem," Millie said. "You actually need to be dead to get his attention."

"But Emma isn't dead," Begonia pointed out.

"She's a novelty," Ginger said. "All males like novelty once in a while. Trust me on that one. Right now, Emma is shiny and new. Every male in town will want to be first to get his fangs, or whatever, into her."

I shuddered. It sounded so crude when she said it.

"Isn't it possible that Demetrius just likes her?" Laurel asked.

Begonia patted her on the head. "You're adorable."

Laurel elbowed her in the ribs. "Don't patronize me."

Ginger clapped her hands. "All right. Let's get

back to potions before Lady Weatherby wanders in and turns us into eels." She lined up three beakers in front of us. One with red liquid, one with silver liquid, and one with orange liquid. "In order to mix this potion correctly, the measurements must be precise. Who has the steadiest hand?"

"Begonia," Sophie, Millie, and Laurel said in unison.

I knew it wasn't me. My hands grew sweaty and shook from the mere act of thinking about doing something I didn't want to do.

Begonia took center stage. "For this transformation potion, we need equal parts of each ingredient." I watched closely as she measured and poured each liquid and placed it into a fresh beaker. It bubbled and fizzed as the liquids merged together.

"Now you need to focus your will and recite the incantation," Ginger reminded her.

Begonia inhaled deeply and rubbed her hands together in an effort to focus. She waved a hand around the top of the container and muttered the relevant rhyme.

"Voila," Begonia said, once she'd finished. "How do we test it?"

Ginger propped her butt cheek on the edge of the table. "We need a volunteer, of course."

"Does it need to be one of us?" Millie asked. "Can't we bring in a dwarf or something?"

Ginger flashed her a look of disapproval. "You know perfectly well that we're not allowed to test our magic on outsiders."

"I don't want to be a frog," Laurel complained. "I don't even like frogs."

"Maybe she didn't choose a frog," I said. "Maybe this potion will turn you into a fluffy bunny."

Laurel looked askance at Ginger. "Would I be a fluffy bunny?"

"Only one way to find out," Ginger replied.

Laurel snatched the container from in front of Begonia. "Fine. I'll be the test case today." She drank every drop of the resulting brownish liquid. It looked far less appealing all mixed together.

We backed away from Laurel, watching for signs of transformation. It happened fairly quickly. Her arms and legs shriveled and shrunk and her head turned green before doing the same.

My hands covered my mouth. On the stool sat an adorable green frog. Her tongue darted out and snatched in a fly.

"Ooh," Begonia said, and wrinkled her nose. "Let's not tell her about the fly."

"Won't she remember being in her frog state?" I asked.

"Actually, she will remember, but she's acting on instinct now," Ginger said. "So we'll just not rub her nose in it, okay?" She looked pointedly at the other three witches and they nodded in agreement.

"So how do we get her back?" I asked. "Does the frog need to drink a potion?" That seemed a difficult task.

"No," Ginger said. "Basic transformation spells are limited in time and scope. Begonia mixed this one to only last for two minutes and thirty seconds."

"It's that exact?" I queried.

Ginger glanced at the clock on the wall. "Wait and see."

Sure enough, Laurel returned to us in her human form at the allotted time. She rubbed her mouth furiously and made gagging noises.

"Drink," she demanded. "I need to wash away the taste of fly."

I stifled a laugh.

Ginger summoned a glass of water with her wand and handed it to Laurel. "If you need something stronger, just ask."

"Something to get rid of the germs would be nice," Laurel said. "I don't care how bad it tastes. The thought of a fly pooping in my mouth is too disgusting for words."

The other girls burst into laughter and I couldn't resist joining in.

"So when would you use a potion like this?" I asked. And how? Did witches walk around with a string of vials attached to their belts?

"You wouldn't use it in your daily life, obviously," Ginger said. "You can't go around using magic willy nilly in Spellbound."

"What about in self-defense?" I asked.

"Yes, of course," Ginger said. "Although your wand is always your best defense. Potions aren't as efficient, for obvious reasons." Ginger stopped talking and glanced over our heads. "Speaking of regulations, here's our lovely sheriff now." Her lips formed a tight smile and I got the impression that she wasn't a fan of Sheriff Hugo.

"Sorry to interrupt," the sheriff said. "May I please have a word with Miss Hart?"

Ginger's brow lifted. "Something the coven can help you with, Sheriff?"

"No, this is a matter between Miss Hart and me."

That didn't sound good. I rose from my stool and met the sheriff at the back of the classroom. He crooked a finger at me and I followed him into the hallway.

"How can I help you, Sheriff?" I asked.

"You can't help me," he said. "So please stop trying." He sounded as irritated as he looked.

"It's my job to help Mumford..." I began.

"I'm not talking about Mumford," he spat. "I'm talking about your interrogation of Spellbound citizens. You went to see Darcy Minor about the calendar."

"She's my neighbor," I said. "I figured it was a good opportunity to meet her and ask a few questions."

"It's not your job to ask questions," he said firmly. "I also have it on good authority that you went to the church to speak with Myra. Why?"

I ground the tip of my shoe into the floor. "I was interested in seeing the inside of a church in Spellbound. Is that a crime?"

Sheriff Hugo bent over so that we were nearly nose-to-nose. "Don't push me, Miss Hart. I am telling you right now to keep your wand out of my investigation."

"My wand?" I echoed. I'd only just gotten my wand.

He heaved an exasperated sigh. "It's an expression, Miss Hart."

Oh.

"Promise me you will cease and desist all activities related to the murder investigation."

Bite me. I held up two fingers and crossed my heart. "I promise."

"You're not doing your client any favors by spending so much time researching something that has nothing to do with you. If I were Mumford, I'd be complaining to the council."

"I didn't ask for that job," I said, a little more irately than I intended.

"It's yours nonetheless, so you may as well give it your best." He tipped his hat at me. "Have a nice day, Miss Hart."

He turned and galloped out of the building.

When I turned to go back inside the classroom, I nearly walked smack into Ginger. "Sorry," I mumbled.

"Don't let him give you a hard time," she said. "He's just trying to intimidate you to keep you under his thumb."

I looked into her hazel eyes. "You don't think I should mind my own business?"

She placed a warm hand on my shoulder. "Honey,

witches never mind their own business. It's why we need to learn so many curses."

I laughed and she guided me back into the classroom. It was comforting to know that I had the support of the coven. Maybe they would turn out to be the family I never had. I dashed the thought as quickly as it came. In my experience, no good ever came from hoping for more than I had.

"What was your argument with Gareth about?" I asked. I was in my office with Mumford after class for another pre-trial meeting.

Mumford gave me a sidelong glance. "What argument?"

"Someone said you and Gareth had argued a couple days before he died. Can you tell me anything about that?"

Mumford examined his fingernails, which caused me to catch a glimpse of them. Long and twisted with a greenish tint, it was fair to say my stomach turned over several times in the span of twenty seconds.

"We weren't arguing," he said. "He was in a foul mood and I asked him why. He didn't like sharing personal information and he snapped at me."

Mumford looked me in the eye. "Are we going to focus on my case? I believe the sheriff is investigating Gareth's death, so I would appreciate it if you'd give my defense your full attention."

I immediately felt guilty. He was right. I'd been spending a lot of time researching Gareth's murder—time that should have been spent developing a defense for Mumford's trial, which was imminent.

"Maybe we should postpone your trial until your neck heals," I suggested, gesturing to his bandage. It didn't even look as though he'd changed the dressing since the last time I saw him. Disgusting.

"Why would we do that?" he asked.

I hesitated. How did I explain to him that his wounded neck was off-putting? Simply because justice was supposed to be blind didn't make it true.

"What if you become ill?" I lied. "We haven't gotten the test results yet. The infection could have spread to your bloodstream."

"Didn't Boyd send an owl?" he asked. "My infection is limited to the wound itself."

Oh. Thanks for the update, Boyd.

"The trial has already been postponed because of Gareth," Mumford complained. "I don't want to wait any longer."

"Yes, it was terribly inconsiderate of him to get murdered before he could have you acquitted."

Although Mumford's expression didn't change, I sensed his displeasure. "I mean no disrespect to Gareth, but our lives here must go on. I have no intention of spending decades in prison because of bad timing."

"Surely it wouldn't be decades for jewelry theft," I said, which reminded me that I really needed to bone up on Spellbound sentencing guidelines.

"All crimes here result in lengthy sentences," Mumford said. "Because we're immortals, more or less, and no one can leave town, examples must be made. I'm fortunate not to be facing a death sentence."

Yikes. Would I be defending clients to save them from the electric chair, or whatever the magical equivalent was? That was far above my pay grade.

I pushed away thoughts of Gareth and the death penalty. Mumford deserved my full attention. "All right, Mumford. Let's go through the questions again. This time, when you answer, try not to sound surly."

"I don't sound surly," he objected, sounding mighty surly.

"Where were you on the morning of the third?" I asked.

"I was at home. Alone."

No alibi. "And what were you doing there?"

"What I always do in the morning. Sleep."

Must be nice. "And what time did you leave your house?"

"My home is not a house," he said. "It's an abandoned mine beneath Donder Mountain."

That sounded depressing. Made me glad I didn't have to pay him any home visits. "And what time did you leave your abandoned mine...er, your home?"

He shifted in his seat. "I believe it was around eleven. I was hungry and decided to walk into town."

"How far do you live from town?"

"About ten miles."

"Ten miles?" I sputtered. "You walk twenty miles round-trip when you come to town?"

"When I choose to walk, yes. It's quite pleasant, actually." He held up an elongated foot. "Goblin feet are different from human feet. We're designed for rough terrain."

"So you chose to walk that day. Why?"

"The sun was shining and I was in a rather good mood."

"Why were you in a good mood?"

"Does it matter?" he asked, uncertain.

"I'd like to know."

He studied me. "Because you're a gossip like your harpy neighbors or because it's relevant?"

I stared right back at him, goiter or no goiter. "I ask the questions here, Mumford. You would do well to remember that."

He gave a tiny smile. "Will you be this feisty in the courtroom?"

I folded my arms across my chest. "If I need to be."

"Good. Gareth wasn't feisty enough for my taste. He tended to let things go."

"No one ever accused me of being someone to let things go." I believe the expression my boss often used was 'like a dog with a bone.' I briefly wondered who had taken over my caseload. Were they working as hard as I had to help their clients? I guess it didn't matter anymore. Not to me.

"Who do you think stole the jewelry?" I asked.

Mumford looked taken aback. "How should I know?"

"Everyone in this town seems to have opinions about the residents. The only reason you're on trial is because you were unlucky enough to find a diamond. If you hadn't, who would the sheriff be investigating?"

Mumford rubbed his chin thoughtfully. "Probably Underkoffler. Or I wouldn't put it past Deacon to stage the whole thing just to gain the town's sympathy."

"Okay, who's Underkoffler?" The name sounded familiar.

"Piotr Underkoffler. He's a vampire who runs the main funeral home."

Oh, right. Best avoided, according to Begonia and Sophie.

"The town undertaker has a bad reputation?" I asked.

"He was accused of looting coffins a few years ago, but no charges were filed." Mumford gave me a disgusted look.

"And Deacon?"

"He's the dwarf who owns the jewelry store. He's always looking for attention. He used to be in that stupid calendar every year until the harpies took it over. Then they only wanted 'hot' males, whatever that means." He shook his head. "I wouldn't be surprised if he staged this whole robbery just so everyone would notice him."

Seemed unlikely.

"Did Gareth look into either of these guys?" I asked. "Or Sheriff Hugo?"

Mumford laughed bitterly. "Certainly not Sheriff Hugo. He decided on me as soon as he found his so-called evidence. Then he didn't have to bother hunting down suspects and could spend more time at the Horned Owl, hitting on the staff."

"And Gareth? What did he think?" I saw no mention of Mumford's theories in the file.

"Piotr Underkoffler is a vampire. Those guys stick together no matter what. And he didn't think the motive for Deacon was persuasive enough." I didn't disagree, but I owed it to Mumford to look into it.

"I'll have a word with Deacon," I said. It had to be soon, since I was running out of time.

"Thank you," Mumford said primly.

"One more question," I said. "What's the point of anyone stealing in this town? You can't sell stolen goods without someone recognizing them because everyone's trapped here. A thief would get caught eventually, right?"

"Not a smart one," Mumford replied. "Spellbound is full of magic, remember. All you'd need is access to the right magic and you'd easily cover your tracks."

I hadn't considered that. The whole magic angle was still new to me.

"It's been a productive meeting, Mumford. I have class shortly and then hopefully I'll speak to Deacon and Underkoffler."

"Learning anything good today?" he asked. "Like how to magically acquit your client?"

I mustered a smile. "Mostly how to avoid Lady Weatherby without her noticing."

"She's a rather difficult woman."

"And a tough teacher," I said. "She won't let me use my wand in class until I can prove I'm not an idiot." I paused. "I'm not sure that I can."

"Her standards are known to be ridiculously high," he said sympathetically. "That's why so many witches fail training the first time around. She wants her coven to be perfect."

"Well, I've never been perfect," I said. "And I have no intention of starting now." I stopped and thought about my statement. "What I mean is..."

"No worries, Miss Hart," Mumford said, and stood to pat me on the shoulder. "I understand. Good luck."

"Thanks, if I can get through the class without injuring myself or anyone else, I'll consider it a success."

CHAPTER 11

CLASS WAS NOT A SUCCESS. And by that, I mean I did not get through the session without injuring someone. Naturally, that someone had to be Lady Weatherby. It wasn't my fault, though. She insisted on giving me the inflammatory spell. How was I supposed to know that it could set a person's hair on fire? I thought it inflicted someone with sore muscles.

Thankfully, Laurel was quick on the draw and used a water spell to douse the flames before any real harm was done. I watched in awe as a stream of water spouted from the tip of the young girl's wand and splashed Lady Weatherby's sizzling head. Smoke began to emanate from her black hair. At least it wasn't steam out of her ears.

"Miss Hart," Lady Weatherby said, raking her

fingers through her singed hair. "Please return Begonia's wand immediately."

I handed over the wand and returned to my seat, deflated. I was so sure today would be better. I had no reason to believe that, though, other than I wanted to.

Begonia clapped me on the shoulder. "We've all done it," she whispered.

Really? They'd all set the teacher's hair on fire? I found that difficult to believe.

"Miss Hart, you seem preoccupied," Lady Weatherby said. "Perhaps if you could focus on spells, you might avoid disastrous results."

I covered my face with my hands. "The truth is I am preoccupied, Lady Weatherby. It's hard to care about inflammatory spells when you have a client on the hook for a crime he didn't commit and a dead undead guy whose killer hasn't been identified."

Lady Weatherby was silent for a moment and I peeked at her between my fingers. "I see," she said finally. "I imagine that is quite a burden to bear."

Slowly, I moved my hands away from my face. Was she actually sympathizing with me? Was she capable of it?

"Are there any spells I could use?" I asked. "Truth serum or something that reveals deception?"

Lady Weatherby sat on the edge of her desk. "If it were that simple, my dear, there would be no need for you, would there?"

"But there must be magic that's useful in this situation," I insisted. "I mean, who cares if I can set your hair on fire? No offense," I added quickly.

"None taken." She steepled her fingers, thinking. "You are correct. There is magic that's useful for investigations, however, it tends not to be used. Not by Gareth or Sheriff Hugo. Nor by their predecessors."

"Why not?"

"Because facts are facts, but magic can be manipulated."

"Ha," I said. "You've never seen the news in the human world. Facts get manipulated every day."

"Magic can be used to show things that are not truly there," she continued. "I can give you a truth potion, but how do you know I didn't tweak it before I gave it to you? Maybe the result will be a distorted truth. As I've said before, part of doing a spell correctly is directing your will. What if your will is to alter the truth?"

She had a point. "I understand. I just feel overwhelmed trying to learn spells and defend my client..." I trailed off.

"And exist in a whole new world?" Lady Weatherby prompted. "I don't envy you, Miss Hart. Your life has, indeed, taken a dramatic turn. Nonetheless, your training here is of the utmost importance. When it comes to you, *that* is my priority." She clapped her hands. "Let us return to the lesson, shall we?"

Considering I'd just set her on fire, it was the nicest she'd ever been to me and I actually felt myself warming to her. Maybe she wasn't so bad after all.

"Miss Hart, try the Shield spell. Use Sophie's wand this time. It's meant for even the clumsiest of witches."

Then again, maybe not.

After class, Begonia insisted on coming with me to visit Deacon.

"He has the loveliest rings in his shop." She extended a hand and I noticed a square-cut emerald glittering on her ring finger. "This was a gift from there, I think. At least it's marked with Deacon's signature 'D.'"

"I thought you didn't have a boyfriend."

"He's not my boyfriend," she said, and sighed happily. "He's a secret admirer."

"That's quite a healthy dose of admiration," I said. The ring was stunning. I wasn't sure how valuable an emerald like that was in Spellbound, but in the human world, it was worth thousands of dollars.

We entered Deacon's Stones and I immediately recognized Deacon, not because I'd seen him before but because he looked exactly like the dwarf I'd pictured in my mind. Thank you, *Lord of the Rings*.

"Good afternoon, ladies," he said brightly. Okay, so he was missing the heavy Scottish brogue. I could live with that.

"Good afternoon, Deacon," Begonia said. "This is my new friend, Emma Hart. She'd like to ask you a few questions."

I caught the flash of recognition in his dark eyes. "You're defending that goblin, aren't you?" he asked. Gone was his sunny demeanor.

I shrugged. "Being a public defender means you don't get to choose your clients." I figured if I didn't spring to Mumford's defense, Deacon might be more willing to talk to me.

He grunted in response. "So what do you need to know?"

As I opened my mouth to speak, Begonia rested her hands on the counter to admire the jewelry behind the glass. Deacon nearly had a stroke right in front of us. His face turned beet red and he clutched his chest.

"Where did you get that ring?" he choked out.

Begonia held it up for closer inspection. "It *is* one of yours, isn't it? I thought so." She seemed pleased, completely missing Deacon's tone.

He gripped her hand and pulled it closer.

"Hey," she said and wrenched back her hand.

"That's one of the stolen pieces," he said. "It's on the list I gave to Sheriff Hugo."

"That's impossible," Begonia said. "My secret admirer gave it to me."

"Well, who's your secret admirer?" he demanded.

She gave him a disappointed look. "If I knew, it wouldn't be a secret now, would it?"

"How was the ring delivered to you?" I asked.

Begonia appeared thoughtful. "By owl," she said finally.

"What did the owl look like?" Deacon asked.

"She's tawny with the most gorgeous green eyes."

"She should be easy to find," Deacon said.

"Of course she is. She's at my house." Begonia shook her head. "The secret admirer used my owl to deliver the ring."

Deacon and I sighed in exasperation.

"Was there a note?" I asked. "How do you know the ring was meant for you?"

"Of course there was a note," Begonia said. "It said, 'Dearest Begonia, A token of my adoration. Thank you for being a breath of fresh air in Spellbound. Yours, X.'"

"Where's the note now?" I asked. "Maybe we can have a handwriting analysis done."

"Oh, no. That isn't possible."

Deacon rolled his eyes. "Why not?"

"I accidentally incinerated it."

"You accidentally..." Deacon let loose a string of curses. "How? How does one accidentally incinerate a love letter?"

"Sophie and I were practicing wandwork—the inflammatory spell that you did today, actually—and I let Sophie use my wand."

"So technically, Sophie accidentally incinerated it," I pointed out. That made more sense.

"I'd shown it to her and left it sitting out when we practiced," Begonia said. "It was my fault."

I gave her a sympathetic look. "I'm afraid the ring will need to go into evidence."

"And then back to me once the trial is over," Deacon said.

Begonia fought back tears. "It's such a beautiful

ring." She drew a steadying breath. "It was nice to feel appreciated for a change, you know?"

I smoothed her hair. "I appreciate you, Begonia. You've been one of the nicest, most generous people I've met in Spellbound. I'm sorry I can't buy you a ring."

"That's okay," she sniffed, and twisted the ring from her finger. "It doesn't mean as much anymore, knowing it was stolen."

She handed me the ring. "I'll make sure this gets catalogued into evidence," I told Deacon.

"Thank you," he said, and patted Begonia's hand. "I'm sorry I was irritable with you. It's not your fault. I can see why he gave it to you. You're one of the prettiest witches in the whole town. Everyone says so."

Begonia's face brightened. "Really?"

Deacon and I nodded.

"Thanks." She seemed happier now.

"Is there anything you can tell me about the burglary that you might have forgotten to tell Gareth or the sheriff?" I asked Deacon.

"No. All the information should be in the file."

"Were you annoyed not to be included in Darcy Minor's annual calendar?" I asked.

His expression clouded over. "That stupid calendar? No, why would I care about a thing like that?"

"From what I understand, you used to be included. Mr. November, was it? Ever since Darcy took over, she's chosen to go in another direction."

He shrugged his thick shoulders. "I understand. The whole point is to raise money. If a dwarf like me isn't going to attract the buyers, how can I object?"

All things considered, he seemed like a reasonable guy.

"Thanks for your time, Deacon," I said. "By the way, do me a favor. If the sheriff asks whether I spoke to you, would you mind telling a small fib?"

Deacon chuckled. "He doesn't like people stepping on his hooves."

"I noticed."

"When you're in the market for a nice piece of jewelry," he said, "you know where to find me."

The likelihood of that happening was somewhere between Magpie getting adopted and me breaking free of the Spellbound curse. My luck was no better here than it had been in the human world.

"Remind me never to go to a jewelry store with you again," Begonia said as we left. "You're bad luck."

"You have no idea," I said. As much as I wanted to laugh it off, I couldn't. Between Mumford's case and Gareth's murder, nothing seemed the least bit funny.

CHAPTER 12

I WAS apprehensive about going to see Piotr Underkoffler, but I promised Mumford I would follow up on his lead. I owed my client that much. Aside from the fact that Underkoffler was a vampire with a bad reputation, he was also the town undertaker. Funeral homes creeped me out as a rule.

The exterior of the building reminded me of a mini mansion. The front porch was supported by Greek-style columns and the double doors at the front looked over-the-top shiny and expensive. I stepped into the grand marble lobby. I suppose if this were my final party, I would want to go out in style too.

Underkoffler spotted me the moment I stepped inside. He was short and slight, with greasy, dark hair and the pale skin often associated with vampires. I hadn't noticed the pale skin of the other vampires I'd met, but that was probably because I'd met them in the middle of the night on a golf course. Hard to get a good look at somebody's complexion under the dim light of the stars.

"Hi there," I said. "You must be Piotr Underkoffler."

He smiled, displaying his fangs. "I am," he said. "I take it you are the new witch in town. What's your name again?" He snapped his fingers, thinking. "Anna Hertz, is it?"

I could tell by the expression on his face that he knew perfectly well what my name was. He was playing a game and it immediately rubbed me the wrong way.

"Emma," I said, mustering my friendliest tone. "Emma Hart."

"How can I help you today, Miss Hart? It's a bit premature to be shopping here, one would think." Although he looked a bit giddy at the prospect. The undertaker definitely gave me the heebie-jeebies.

"I'm here to ask your involvement in the jewelry theft," I said. "The one Mumford has been accused of."

Underkoffler focused on me. His icy gaze seemed to penetrate my soul. I could easily picture him feeding on the blood of the innocents. He was probably one of the main reasons this town was cursed in the first place. Maybe he tried to bite the enchantress while she was in town and she didn't quite appreciate it.

"I don't know anything about the jewelry heist." He didn't seem angry or insulted that I insinuated his involvement.

"Are you sure about that?" I asked, and decided to push the envelope a little further. "After all, Gareth was your friend. Maybe he found out that you were the real culprit and you killed him to keep him quiet."

He continued to fixate on me. "I like your style, Emma Hart. If you ever grow bored with this public defender business, come and see me."

When pigs fly. Wait. Did pigs fly here? I'd have to check.

"Do you think Mumford stole the jewels?" I asked.

"I have no idea. It's nothing to do with me. That's the beauty of being a narcissist. If I'm not at the center of it, I just don't give a damn."

Well, glad we got that sorted. "I visited a few of your friends at the country club the other day," I said. "Do you ever golf with them?" I was curious to see if the other vampires were willing to socialize with Underkoffler. It was one thing to protect your own, but if they willingly hung around with him, that suggested he was socially acceptable.

"I don't care for golf," he said and sniffed. "It's a tedious game and the clothes are hideous."

He didn't really answer my question. "Are you the only funeral home in town?" I asked. A monopoly on corpses. A vampire's wet dream.

"Not every deceased member of the community chooses a proper burial," he said. "Some people don't like the attention."

I was hesitant to point out that most of them wouldn't be aware of the attention, given their situation. "I understand Gareth's service was held here."

"Of course. He was one of us. And I didn't charge his estate any money." He appeared quite proud of himself.

"One last question, Mr. Underkoffler. Do you have any theories on who may have killed Gareth?"

"You, too?" He sighed heavily. "I've already spoken with Sheriff Hugo at length about both the jewelry heist and Gareth's murder. I know nothing about any of it, no matter what anyone thinks." He crossed his arms and huffed.

"Please don't take offense," I said. "I'm simply trying to help my client."

He smiled again, reminding me of his deadly teeth. "You do so remind me of Gareth, saying things like that. He was always trying to help. It was one of his most annoying qualities. That, and his loud socks."

Loud socks? I assume he meant colorful. I'd have to rifle through the dresser drawers and see what he meant.

I left Underkoffler's funeral home feeling mildly unsettled. Although I'd been afraid to meet vampires when I first arrived, he was the first one to actually make me uncomfortable. The whole time we were speaking, I felt like he was staring at my neck. It reminded me of the way a man might let his gaze linger on my chest for too long, not that there was too much to ogle. For some men, any boobs would do.

My negative feelings aside, I wasn't sure that Underkoffler had anything to do with the jewelry heist or Gareth's murder. There didn't appear to be a motive. He seemed to be doing well financially, given his monopoly on funerals in town. I knew from experience that criminals didn't always steal because they needed the money, though. I definitely couldn't see a reason why he would want to kill Gareth. He may be a social pariah, but Gareth seemed to look out for him for some reason. There was no discernible reason why Underkoffler would turn on him. In fact, of all the people in town I'd met so far, Underkoffler seemed to be the one worse off as a result of Gareth's murder. If he were a different sort of vampire, maybe he'd be more interested in helping solve the murder. I guess he wasn't kidding about being a narcissist. He wasn't the one murdered, therefore, he wasn't interested in solving the case. Note to self: no narcissists as friends.

As I walked away from the grand funeral home, I heard the gentle sound of wings flapping behind me. I turned around to see Lucy in mid-air.

"Miss Hart," she exclaimed. "What a lovely surprise to run into you. How are you getting on?"

"Hi Lucy," I said. "Very busy between lessons and Mumford's case, but otherwise okay."

Lucy gave me a sly smile. "I understand you've been doing a little investigating on your own. It seems to have ruffled more than a few feathers."

Did she mean actual feathers or metaphorical feathers? In this town, I wasn't too sure.

I feigned innocence. "Oh? Am I causing any problems?"

"Not as far as I'm concerned," she said. "We need more community-minded residents in Spellbound. Sometimes we seem to forget that the entire reason we're trapped here is because we mistreated someone. It's important that we strive to do better and look out for one another."

I smiled at Lucy. I expected fairies to be sweet, and it was nice to know this one actually was. I wasn't so sure about Mayor Knightsbridge. Even though she was the mayor, she struck me as serious and inflexible.

"I understand the trial is coming up," Lucy said. "Do you think you'll be ready?"

"I sure hope so," I said. "I don't want my first case to result in jail time for my client. I already feel like I've started off on the wrong foot here."

"Not with everyone," Lucy said vaguely. Although her expression suggested she had more to say on the matter, she didn't elaborate. "How's your progress with witch training?"

I pulled my Tiffany blue wand from my bag and she squealed with delight.

"That is stunning." Lucy zipped down beside me to admire the wand more closely. "I swear witch wands are so much nicer than fairy wands."

"But yours has glitter," I pointed out.

"Yours is so sophisticated." Lucy stared glumly at her own wand. "Mine is made for a child."

I hadn't looked in the fairy section of Wands-A-Plenty. "Can't you ask Alaric for a better selection?"

"To be honest, it never occurred to me. Fairy wands have always been different from witch wands." She flashed a bright smile. "That's a great idea, though. See? You're making a difference already, Emma. Sometimes an outsider's perspective is just what a place needs."

I was glad Lucy thought so, but I had the sense not everyone in Spellbound would agree.

"Let me know when you're ready to go shopping again," Lucy said. "I'd love to take you."

"Thanks." I hesitated. "By the way, any chance you know someone interested in adopting a cat?"

She looked at me askance. "If you're talking about Gareth's four-legged monstrosity, the answer is no. You can always take it to Paws and Claws. At least there are other animals there for the cat to interact with."

Magpie's idea of interacting with other animals probably included a lot of hissing and an unhealthy dose of urination.

"Thanks, I'll think about it." I wouldn't feel right about bringing Magpie to the rescue center. Gareth's house was his home, whether I liked it or not. We'd simply have to find a way to co-exist.

"Where are you off to now?" Lucy asked.

"Gareth's house," I said. "To feed the four-legged monstrosity."

"It's your house now, silly," she said.

Maybe so, but it didn't feel like mine. Not in its current state anyway. I thought about the blue and yellow pot I'd placed on the windowsill. Right now it was the only reflection of me in the house. That would have to change soon…but not until Gareth's killer was brought to justice. There was a part of me that felt I needed to earn what I'd been given here. If I was honest with myself, it was the real reason I couldn't stop investigating Gareth's murder, despite the sheriff's warnings. If I successfully defended Mumford and helped to solve Gareth's murder, then, and only then, would I feel like I'd earned the right to enjoy the fruits of Gareth's labors.

CHAPTER 13

AFTER ANOTHER RESTLESS night and another morning spent memorizing every detail in Mumford's file, I wasn't looking forward to Beginner Spell Casting. It was hard to focus your will when your will was half asleep.

"We'll have to take you to the Beauty Bar one of these days," Begonia said, when I sat down beside her.

"If I weren't so tired, I'd feel insulted," I replied.

"My facialist has amazing tricks for dark circles under the eyes," she said.

"I think sleep is the amazing trick I'm looking for," I said.

"You're trying too hard to do everything," Sophie interjected. "You need to relax a little."

"If I don't do my job properly, Mumford is the one who will pay the price for it, not me."

I didn't want to burden them with my insomnia issues. Unfortunately, my sleep problems predated my new life in Spellbound.

Lady Weatherby appeared at the front of the class in her usual intimidating fashion. "Good afternoon, witches. I'd intended to review the four basic spells again, but I think a departure is in order. Sometimes it's useful to wander off the beaten path in order to regain one's perspective."

Had she and Lucy been comparing notes? It seemed unlikely that the two of them would be friends. Then again, Lucy absolutely adored Mayor Knightsbridge, so anything was possible.

Lady Weatherby's lips stretched into her version of a smile. "Today might be a good day to test out your wand, Miss Hart."

"Seriously?" I couldn't believe it. Were the training wheels coming off already? Before she could change her mind, I rummaged through my shoulder bag and whipped out my wand in anticipation.

"Begonia, as I recall, you were adept with spells of superficiality last term. Why don't you demonstrate one for us?"

Begonia's shoulders straightened. "Yes, Lady Weatherby." She took her place in front of the class. "Any spell in particular?"

"Your choice."

Wow. Lady Weatherby must have had a shot of generosity in her morning latte. This collaborative approach to learning was not her usual style.

Begonia turned toward me. "This is your lucky day, Emma."

I find that difficult to believe, I thought to myself.

Me too, Sedgwick chimed in from his corner of the room.

No one asked you, I snapped.

Can I please grab her wand and fly off with it just for fun? I know lots of places off the beaten track.

I'll bet. *You will do no such thing.*

Begonia pointed her wand at me and chanted, "Let this spell erase/the stress to Emma's face."

I felt the energy prick my skin, more like a vibration than a pinch.

"Someone get her a mirror," Begonia said excitedly.

Millie thrust a mirror under my nose and my eyes widened at the reflection. The dark circles were gone and my freckles had faded. My complexion was clear and smooth, making my green eyes pop. I could even see little flecks of gold.

I touched my cheek in amazement. Who needed the Beauty Bar when you were friends with talented witches?

"Begonia, that's incredible."

She curtsied and glanced over her shoulder at Lady Weatherby. "Please can I do another? Her hair is crying out for a root spell."

Lady Weatherby rolled her dark eyes. "As you wish. One more and then we'll move on."

Begonia pumped her fist in the air before focusing her attention back on me. She pointed her wand again and said, "Consider it a gift/to give this hair a lift."

I picked up the mirror and gasped. My flat, stringy hair was shiny and full. It was the closest I'd ever come to looking like a Dallas housewife.

"Every witch should feel beautiful," Begonia said.

"I do now," I said. "Thank you."

"All right," Lady Weatherby said, motioning for Begonia to sit down. "Let's try something else. Miss Hart, why don't you take center stage?"

Begonia gave me a supportive squeeze as we passed each other.

"There are other superficiality spells," Lady

Weatherby said. "Obviously Begonia chose ones to improve someone's appearance. As with all spells, there are ones that produce the opposite result."

"I'm going to make someone ugly?" I asked.

"Not necessarily," she replied. "You can choose a spell that mimics an allergic reaction, for example."

"Like a bee sting?"

"Yes. Or a spell that distorts certain features. Makes the nose bigger or the ears larger."

I clutched my wand, thinking hard. Under no circumstances did I want to accidentally distort Lady Weatherby's features. I had to make sure I directed my will in the opposite direction.

"Whenever you're ready, Miss Hart."

I cleared my throat and took a deep breath. Pointing my wand at Millie, I began to chant, "A finger to a ring/A face to a sting."

My fatal error was movement. I was meant to remain in a standing pose, with my feet firmly planted. I knew this the way I knew I needed air to breathe. My brain, however, had other ideas and told my feet to walk toward Millie—probably due to my irrational fear that I'd somehow manage to zap Lady Weatherby anyway.

I lurched forward as the tip of my toe caught on the table leg, and I lost control of the wand. I watched it—in what seemed like slow motion—fly out of my hand and flip through the air. As (bad) luck would have it, the tip of the wand pointed at the door at precisely the moment Sheriff Hugo ducked his head inside. His lips had just parted to speak when the spell took effect. The witches in the room gasped in horror as his cheeks swelled, then his nose, and finally his forehead. If I'd poked his head with a pin, I was sure it would have burst.

"Stars and stones," Laurel breathed.

A heavy silence followed until my wand clattered to the floor, the sound jarring Lady Weatherby into action. She pointed her own wand at Sheriff Hugo and spoke in Latin. Some kind of counterspell, I assumed. Whatever she did, it worked because the sheriff's swollen face began to deflate and his normal features were quickly restored. Despite the fast turnaround, the centaur did not seem happy.

I ran over and picked up my wand.

"Miss Hart," Lady Weatherby seethed. "Please lower your wand."

My hand dropped to my side. "I wasn't going to use it again." I looked back at the sheriff. "I'm sorry. It was an accident."

"You'll have to be better than sorry," Lady Weatherby said. "Sorry doesn't stir the cauldron." She inhaled sharply. "Under the circumstances, I think it would be best if you took a break from witchcraft. It's been rather a lot for you to take in. Perhaps it's a case of too much too soon."

If you ask me, the entire town of Spellbound was a case of too much too soon. No one seemed to care how I was coping with this new life. Some residents had centuries to get used to the idea of living here, not to mention the fact that they already knew they were supernatural creatures. Every bit of this was new to me. Every daily task. I couldn't possibly be a model student right out of the gate. My familiar wasn't even a cat! Yet I was expected to embrace this life because I had no choice. Well, it didn't mean I wasn't going to mourn the life I left behind. Maybe I needed a funeral procession like Gareth's. A red robe to publicly display my grief.

Come on, Sedgwick, I said glumly. *Let's go home.*

Don't worry about them. It will blow over in no time.

"It doesn't matter how long it takes," I said aloud. "I'll still be here either way."

CHAPTER 14

I LEFT the academy with Sedgwick flying above me at a safe distance. He'd made it clear that he didn't like to perch on my shoulder like other owls. He was a snobby little thing, but he was mine.

I was too busy wallowing in self-pity to pay attention to where I was going or I would have avoided walking straight into a solid wall of vampire chest.

"Pardon me," Demetrius said. "Are you all right?"

I was fine, more embarrassed by the fact that my boobs were squashed against his chest mere seconds ago.

"It was my fault," I blurted. "Everything is my fault. The sheriff's ugly face. Gareth's murderer on the loose." I waved my hands in the air. "And

Mumford is probably going to spend eternity in prison because of me."

Demetrius fixed his soulful eyes on me. "You're too pretty to look so shaken up. Why don't you come and have a drink with me? Soothe those fractious nerves of yours."

"I'd like to, but I have to prepare for Mumford's trial." Wow. His eyes were mesmerizing. Could he please stop looking at me like that? It was very...seductive.

"The only part of that sentence I heard was 'I'd like to.'" His smile was smooth and sexy. The sight of his fangs made my heart flutter.

"I suppose I could spare an hour," I said. Or two. He even smelled good. Did vampires have a natural scent? I would've thought that was more of a werewolf thing.

Sedgwick, you can go home.

Are you sure? What if he tries to bite you?

I'll be disappointed if he doesn't.

Witches are weird.

Sedgwick flew off in the direction of the house and I continued to stand there, staring into Demetrius's handsome face.

"The pub is this way," he said, and offered his arm.

The Horned Owl was the rival pub to the Spotted Owl. They were owned by incubi—two brothers. Vampires and certain other residents preferred the Horned Owl, whereas werewolves, sirens, and witches preferred the Spotted Owl.

When we walked in together, every head seemed to swivel in our direction. I wasn't sure if it was the sight of me in the bar, or the sight of me with Demetrius that made them curious.

"You're very popular," he murmured, his breath warm on my neck. I shivered.

"It's probably you. Everybody hates me."

Speaking of residents who hated me, Sheriff Hugo trotted over from his stool at the bar. "Demetrius. Miss Hart."

"Sheriff Hugo. A little early for you, isn't it?" Demetrius asked.

"I'm recovering from an incident," the sheriff said, giving me a pointed look. "Nothing a shot of whiskey fizz can't cure."

"How goes the investigation?" Demetrius asked. "Lord Gilder and the rest of us are quite eager for Gareth's killer to be brought to justice."

"I am well aware," Sheriff Hugo said. "Astrid and I are doing our best, but some folks seem to think they can do a better job."

"Don't worry, Sheriff," I said. "I'm not meddling anymore. I can't seem to do anything right, and that includes crime solving."

"Glad to hear it. Best to leave these things to the professionals." He aimed his index finger at me like a gun and pretended to fire. I was beginning to think he wasn't a centaur after all. What do you call a creature that's part man, part jackass?

Demetrius steered me to a quiet booth at the back of the pub. As we passed the booth in front of ours, a familiar face greeted mine.

"Hello," I said to Daniel. I glanced at his companion, a pretty woman I didn't recognize. Her hair rolled down her shoulders in titian waves and her creamy complexion made me grateful for Begonia's spell.

Daniel seemed equally surprised to see me here with Demetrius. "Hello." He hesitated, taking in my depressed appearance. "Are you okay?"

I smiled weakly. "Define okay."

"Emma, you know Daniel, our heaven-sent resident." Demetrius gestured to the woman. "His date is Teena."

"She's not my date," Daniel said quickly.

Teena smiled at me, unconcerned with Daniel's

outburst. "A pleasure to meet you finally, Emma. I have heard so much about you."

I detected a slight Eastern European accent. How did any of them manage to retain their native accents after so many years? Part of the curse, I guess.

"She's a succubus," Demetrius whispered.

I couldn't remember exactly what a succubus was, except she had something to do with sex. I swallowed hard. Great. Daniel was interested in sex, just not with me. Then again, I was out with a vampire. I wondered what Daniel thought about that. I focused my will on him. Maybe if I could read an owl's mind, I could read an angel's mind, too. After all, they both had wings.

"Emma, are you feeling unwell?" Demetrius asked, sliding a concerned hand around my waist.

"No, why?"

"You look like you're about to be sick."

I smoothed my hair and smiled. Apparently my focused face had a constipated quality to it.

"You are most welcome to join us," Teena said.

"Oh." My gaze shifted from Teena to Daniel. Did he mind? Did he want me to join them?

"If you don't mind, I'd like to get to know Emma without distractions," Demetrius said. He shot Teena a pointed look. "You know how greedy you can be when it comes to male attention."

Teena blew him a kiss. "Fair enough, my love."

I slid into the booth behind them and was acutely aware of Daniel directly behind me. I wasn't sure if I could give Demetrius my full attention with Daniel so close to me.

"If you need any recommendations, just ask," Demetrius said. "I'm sure it must be disconcerting, not knowing what to eat or drink."

His empathy amazed me. Weren't vampires supposed to be cold, callous creatures? Yet here sat Demetrius, able to pinpoint a basic fact that most others had overlooked.

"Thank you, Demetrius," I said. "I would love suggestions."

"Don't let him suggest the rosenberry cocktail," Daniel said, hanging over the back of my seat. "It's potent. He'll be carrying you home after one drink, which is probably his intention."

"Mind your own business, errand boy," Demetrius said. "If you must know, I was going to recommend the house wine with a plate of futzel."

"Errand boy?" I queried.

Demetrius gave a dismissive flick of his fingers.

"You know. Messenger of God." He rolled his dark eyes. Damn, he even made eye rolling sexy.

"I'm keeping an eye on you, Hunt," Daniel said. "Emma's sweet. She doesn't know you like I do."

I was sweet? I couldn't decide if I wanted to be sweet. Did that mean I wasn't sexy?

"Teena looks bored," Demetrius said. "You should probably feed her before she goes in search of someone else."

"She's not feeding on me," Daniel ground out. "We're friends."

"I'll be fine, Daniel," I said. "Thank you for your concern."

Daniel seemed disappointed that I'd brushed him aside. "Shouldn't you be preparing for Mumford's trial?"

I bristled. "I've had a crappy day, and Demetrius was kind enough to bring me here to recharge my very frazzled batteries."

"Anything you want to tell me about?" Daniel asked. Seeing his concerned expression, I softened.

"Lady Weatherby has expelled me from school temporarily. It seems I'm so horrible at witchcraft, I can't even handle the remedial class."

"Oh," Demetrius and Daniel said in unison.

"That is pretty crappy," Daniel agreed. "What happened?"

"It doesn't matter," I said. I was sure the whole town would hear about it before the end of the night anyway. That seemed to be how Spellbound worked.

"If you decide you want to talk about it, you know where to find me," Daniel said.

Actually, I had no clue where to find him, but that wasn't important right now.

Although I heard them get up to leave, I didn't turn around to confirm it. I didn't want to watch Daniel leave with the succubus.

"What did you mean about him feeding her?" I asked. "She's not a vampire."

"No," he said. "More's the pity. She's a demon who relies on sex with men to replenish her strength. The longer she goes without sex, the more haggard she looks and feels. Incubi are the same, just the male form. In fact, Teena's brother owns this place."

I'd need to steer clear of him. I didn't want to 'feed' anyone that way.

"She didn't look haggard to me," I said. "I guess she's been busy stocking up on…food."

Demetrius smiled and I saw that flash of fang again. "Speaking of food, why don't I order for us?"

"Thanks."

I observed him as he walked over to the bar to exchange a few words with the bartender. Was it wrong to stare at a vampire's butt? Demetrius didn't strike me as the type of man who would mind being objectified.

He was back in the booth in a flash, much to my disappointment. I was looking forward to watching the return journey.

"So you have some kind of speed superpower?" I asked.

"We can travel at high speeds," he said.

"What about flying?"

"Only in bat form," he said. "And we rarely do that. Too many owls here to risk taking the form of a rodent."

I thought of Sedgwick, who probably wouldn't hesitate to make a snack of bat-shaped Demetrius.

"Can you jump high?" I asked.

"Yes, and we're strong. Our golf clubs are magically enhanced so we don't break them when we play." He tapped his elegant fingers on the table. "We also have impressive stamina, in case you were wondering. Any more questions for me?"

I cleared my throat, feeling the heat rush to my cheeks. "Not at this time, Your Honor," I joked.

"Now it's my turn," he said, just as a server arrived. She set down two wine glasses and a plate of something that looked like a pretzel and cracker combo. I guess that was futzel. "Thank you, Sasha."

"Anything for you, Dem." She gave him a sultry wink before retreating.

"Is she a succubus too?" I asked.

"No, she's simply an incorrigible flirt. Sasha is a dryad."

"A tree nymph?"

He seemed impressed. "That's right. Now about you..."

I took a sip of wine. "Delicious," I said. I wasn't exactly an expert since my wine generally came out of a box, but I always had an opinion. "Before you grill me, can I just talk to you a little more about Gareth?"

He leaned back against the booth. "I thought you told the sheriff you were done investigating?"

"I meant it when I said it." Twenty minutes ago. "A woman is entitled to change her mind."

He grinned. "That she is. So what would you like to know?"

I told him about my conversations with Alison, Myra, and the harpies. "The sheriff still has no leads, and neither do I."

"And this bothers you?"

"How can it not?" Although I spoke more heatedly than I intended, Demetrius didn't seem bothered. "I took his house, his job, even his cat."

"Calling that thing a cat is an insult to cats."

"Even so, I'm having a hard time stepping into his shoes while his murderer runs free. It feels horribly unjust."

"So what do you need from me? I want Gareth's murder solved as much as anyone. He was a dear friend."

"Is there anything else you can tell me about the days leading up to his death?" I asked.

Demetrius leaned forward. "I really wish I had the magic answer, but I don't. And you shouldn't beat yourself up over it either, although I must admit, I find your intrepid nature quite attractive."

A thin man stumbled over to our table and slapped his hands down. "You look fabulous in that outfit," he slurred.

"Nice to see you, Ricardo," Demetrius said. He cast a sidelong glance at me. "I take it you shopped at Ready-to-Were."

"Impeccable taste," Ricardo shouted.

Sasha approached the table with a tray of shot

glasses. “Ricardo asked me to bring these.” She set a shot glass in front of each of us.

Ricardo picked up his drink and toasted me. “To a fantastic addition to the community.” He threw back the amber liquid and slammed the glass onto the table. “It tastes like Christmas is coming in my mouth.”

I cringed. “What is it?”

Demetrius lifted his glass and sniffed. “An Evergreen Blast.” He tipped his back slowly and exhaled. “Nice.”

“You will love this. I promise you.” Ricardo gesticulated wildly. I wondered how long he’d been drinking. I hadn’t even noticed him when we came in.

I raised the drink to my lips and glugged it down. He was right; it did taste like Christmas. Less than a minute later, my head went fuzzy.

“I should have warned you that it’s strong,” Demetrius said.

Ricardo shoved in beside me. “Do you like music? You must come out for karaoke one night.”

“Ricardo loves to sing,” Demetrius said. “Just don’t get up there on a night when Alison shows up. She blows everybody out of the water.”

“I’ll bet.”

"How are you liking my clothes?" Ricardo asked. His breath smelled like a pine forest. Considering his inebriated state, I could think of worse things it could smell like.

"I love them." It was true. I did. "When I start making money, I will definitely be back."

He clapped his hands giddily. "Wonderful. Demetrius, you must come in again soon. I have a new collection that will fit your body like a second skin."

"I'd be happy to come by this week."

"Excellent." He leaned his head on my shoulder. "You come by again, too. I love my customers."

Demetrius gently pushed his head off my shoulder. "Sometimes too much. Go home, Ricardo. It's time for bed."

Bed sounded pretty good to me right now. When my body decided it was time for sleep, I didn't argue.

"I think I'm ready to call it a night," I said groggily.

"Just one more round of shots," Ricardo begged. "You will sleep like a ferret, I promise you."

I wasn't sure whether sleeping like a ferret was what I wanted, but I soldiered on for another hour before Demetrius drove us both home. Since it was Ricardo's car, he dropped me off first.

"Seems that your unlucky day was a lucky one for me," he said, helping me up the steps to the front door. "I'd like to do this again another time. When you're not so busy cursing the sheriff."

Oops. I must have confessed at some point during the evening.

"Thanks for a fun night," I said.

His lips brushed lightly against mine. "The pleasure was all mine."

I shivered happily before slipping inside.

Did he bite you? Sedgwick asked as I made my way up the stairs.

"Close enough," I replied, and crawled into bed.

CHAPTER 15

THE WINE at the Horned Owl must have been fortified because I woke up with a killer hangover. Then again, maybe it was the third shot of Evergreen Blast that did me in. My head throbbed and the inside of my mouth was full of cotton. Not what I needed when I had to work on Mumford's case.

I dragged myself out of bed and into the shower. Sedgwick observed me from his post, staying quiet. Very considerate of him, since every sound in my head was like a drumbeat right now.

After getting dried and dressed, I had a sip of water. Slow rehydration was the key.

You have mail, Sedgwick said.

I went downstairs and opened the front door just in time to see an owl fly away. I glanced down to the porch and saw a small package. I brought it inside and unwrapped it.

There's a note, Sedgwick said.

I unfolded the note. "To help with the hangover," I read aloud. "It's from Demetrius."

I opened the package to reveal a small vial of green liquid.

It's a tonic, Sedgwick told me.

"How thoughtful," I said. The color reminded me of a kale smoothie. I popped off the lid and drank it down.

You're very trusting, Sedgwick said disapprovingly.

"You don't like Demetrius?"

He's a vampire. I'm reserving judgment.

"Your choice." I stretched my arms overhead. "I feel better already. That stuff is amazing." I looked at Sedgwick. "So if I want to send a thank you note, I write it out and give it to you?"

If an owl could roll his eyes, I swear it totally just happened. *If you wish.* He titled his head at a ridiculous angle. *This isn't going to become a habit, is it?*

"What?"

Passing notes between the two of you. I don't want to be the intermediary in a love letter campaign.

"That's your job, Sedgwick, remember? To deliver my mail. Never mind the content of the letters." I scribbled a clever thank you note and placed it in Sedgwick's beak. "Off you go." I opened the front door and shooed him away. He nearly flew straight into Alison.

"Ack," she cried, and ducked quickly as he skimmed the top of her head.

"Alison," I exclaimed.

"Sorry to come without sending a message first," she said. "Can I come in?"

"Of course." I stepped aside.

In the foyer, Alison looked me over. "You look pretty good for someone who closed down the Horned Owl with Demetrius Hunt."

"You heard about that?"

"The gossipmongers here consider it their civic duty to pass along such information." She heaved a sigh. "You'll learn soon enough."

"I wish they'd pass along more important information." Like who stole the jewels from Deacon's shop or who killed Gareth. "What brings you here?"

"I've been doing a lot of thinking since you came to see me."

Oh? Was there a confession coming? I hoped not, because I'd already ruled her out as a suspect.

She chewed her lip, her gaze dropping to the

hardwood floor. "I told you that we fought all the time, but I didn't say why."

"I thought you just didn't get along."

She hugged herself. "There was more to it than that. I thought maybe he was interested in someone else because he didn't seem interested in me. I even tried to make him jealous by flirting with a hot werewolf at a wedding, but he didn't bat an eye. It pissed me off."

I hated to ask—"Were you sleeping together?"

"On occasion," she admitted. "But it had become less frequent. That's when I decided there might be another woman. I even followed Teena one night to see if she was feeding on him, draining him of his sexual energy."

"And was she?"

Alison shook her head. "I had lunch with Althea to see if she knew anything. She was as clueless as me, which didn't surprise me, but I was feeling increasingly desperate."

"You don't think he was involved with Althea, do you?" She was very attractive for a woman with snakes on her head.

"No, definitely not. Gareth hated snakes. Their relationship was very perfunctory. I don't think they spoke about their personal lives to each other very often."

Alison breathed in the aroma of the house. "It feels good to be back here. I kinda miss this musty old house." She surveyed the foyer. "I guess you've been too busy to make any decorative changes."

"It's a work in progress."

She gestured to the staircase. "What happened there? Did your owl take out the banister like he nearly took out my head?"

I glanced at the broken banister. "No, it was like that when I came."

Alison looked thoughtful. "Really? It must have happened very recently. I was here the week he died and it was intact."

We both reacted at the same time.

"The murder weapon," I said. "We need to find the missing support post."

"But Gareth was found in the forest."

"I'll bet you anything he was killed right here."

Alison stared at the floor. "So the murderer must be someone strong enough to carry Gareth's limp body all the way to the forest and smart enough to dispose of the murder weapon."

In Spellbound, that didn't rule out many residents.

I snapped my fingers. "The fireplace." I rushed into the adjacent living room and Alison followed me.

"When I first arrived, the fireplace showed signs of use." I dropped to my knees in front of the hearth. "I thought it was odd because the weather was so mild, but then I figured maybe a vampire was always chilly."

Alison kneeled beside me and grabbed a nearby poker. "It's the perfect place to destroy a piece of wood."

"For once, I really wish I could communicate with cats. Magpie probably knows the whole story."

Alison eyed me curiously. "You can't speak to your cat? I thought that was a witch trait."

"Apparently, it's a witch trait for this coven." I shrugged. "My coven is different, hence different abilities." Some abilities I probably wasn't even aware of yet. It was going to be an interesting year.

She pushed around the ashes. "Something was definitely burned here."

And thank goodness Bernadette's crew did a substandard job of cleaning this level of the house. I guess Kendra was going to be my chosen fairy cleaner from now on.

"But there's no way of knowing if it was just kindling in here," I said.

"This is Spellbound, Emma. There's always a way." She stood and dusted off her knees. "I'll have Sheriff Hugo send someone around to collect the ashes. They'll be able to analyze it for evidence of the support post from the banister."

"Even if the remains are here, will we be able to show it was the murder weapon?" Would there be vampire DNA on it?

"If whatever is in these charred remains was used to kill Gareth, the sheriff's office will be able to tell. Their forensics team includes a fairy and a witch."

Huh. I didn't know that.

"This is great, Alison," I said. "We may have found the scene of the murder as well as the weapon." Put that in your finger gun and smoke it, Sheriff Hugo.

It didn't help me solve Mumford's case, but at least we were one step closer to finding Gareth's murderer. At this point, I'd take anything I could get.

Sheriff Hugo joined his forensics team at the house.

"I thought you were staying out of this," the sheriff said, his arms folded across his human chest.

"I thought I was, too," I said. "I can't help that

Alison noticed the staircase." I fixed him with a disapproving stare. "Didn't you search Gareth's home after his body was discovered?"

"Of course we did," the sheriff huffed. "How could we have known the breakage was recent? It wasn't as though he had a roommate to ask."

No, he didn't. And Magpie wasn't anyone's familiar, so the forensics team witch couldn't have interrogated him.

"What about the fireplace?" I asked. "No one thought it was odd that Gareth had used it? Other than the kitchen, it seems like he rarely used this floor at all. Why use the fireplace then?"

Sheriff Hugo's expression was the epitome of annoyed.

"Listen up, Nancy Shrew," he snapped. "I'm not interested in your critique of this investigation. You're new here and I'll give you a free pass. This time."

"You've heard of Nancy Drew?" I asked.

"In case you haven't noticed, we have a library and a bookstore in Spellbound. We're not savages."

"There are books from the human world?" I knew where I'd be heading as soon as Mumford's case was finished.

"There are summoning spells that allow for

books to be imported." He wagged a finger at me. "Before you get any ideas, every spell like that has to go through the proper procedure."

I turned my eyes skyward. *Dear Daniel's brothers in heaven.* "You seriously love your red tape around here."

"We can't allow magic users to run roughshod over this town," he said, and I suddenly pictured him wearing a gold star pin and a holster.

"I hardly think summoning a copy of *Pride and Prejudice* will wreak havoc on supernatural civilization."

"Rules are rules, Miss Hart. You'll learn."

I kept hearing that I'd learn. I wasn't sure if I wanted to. Not when learning seemed to imply finding out about things that annoyed me.

I stood out of the way as the sheriff's team removed the debris from the hearth. Sedgwick flew in during the bustling activity.

What happened?

I filled him in telepathically, so that Sheriff Hugo didn't hear me refer to him as a jackass.

I leave for half an hour and all hell breaks loose.

What can I say, Sedgwick? Where I go, trouble follows.

Then perhaps you should stop courting it. He

dropped a note into my hand. *From your fanged paramour.*

As I unfolded the note, I felt like I was back in school, passing notes in class with my ninth grade crush. I probably hadn't held a guy's interest since then.

I sighed as I read the saucy note and blushed. Demetrius wasn't Daniel, but he was one handsome distraction.

"Anything you care to share, Miss Hart?" Sheriff Hugo asked.

I crumpled the note and stuffed it into my pocket. "It's personal. Nothing to do with the investigation."

"From your new friend, Mr. Hunt?"

My expression hardened. "That's none of your business."

"Stay out of my business, and I'll stay out of yours."

"Gladly."

I breathed a sigh of relief when the sheriff gathered his team and left. I needed to get back to the office and go through my notes one more time. I'd prepared a few questions for Mumford, and I wanted to make sure I'd covered every possible angle. Criminal law was still new to me, and I didn't want my inexperience to show. Mumford deserved better than that.

Now that we were one step closer to finding Gareth's killer, I felt a surge of optimism. I didn't need to find the real thief in order to get Mumford acquitted. I just needed to prove that it wasn't Mumford. For the first time since my arrival, I couldn't wait to get to the office.

CHAPTER 16

"So how's Demetrius Hunt?" Daniel asked. He was sitting on the front step of my porch when I arrived home from the office. I was going to need to look into a mode of transport soon because my feet were killing me. I wasn't lucky enough—or unlucky enough—to have goblin feet.

"With everything going on in my life, that's the question you want to ask me?" I brushed past him and pulled out my key to unlock the door.

He hopped up and joined me at the door. "Aren't you going to ask me about Teena?"

"No need. Demetrius told me all about her." I left it at that.

"She and I have been friends for a long time," he said.

"Friends with benefits?"

He wore a blank expression. "All friends have benefits," he said. "Otherwise, what would be the point of them?"

So that wasn't an expression here. Another mental note to add to the ever-growing list.

"You came all the way over here to tell me that you and Teena have a historical friendship?" I pushed open the door and stepped into the foyer.

"And to find out whether Demetrius tried anything with you. You can't trust him."

I whirled around and faced him. "Because he's a vampire?"

"No, because he's a player."

"So what? I heard *you* were a player."

My remark went unnoticed. He was too busy noticing the tidy state of the main floor. "What happened here?"

Usually you ask what happened when a room is a mess, not when it looks pristine.

I counted on my fingers. "Fairy cleaners, the sheriff's forensics team, Magpie and Sedgwick had a knock-down-drag-out fight..."

"The owl and the pussycat don't get along?"

"They're working on their relationship." Working on destroying it.

"So when are you going to paint in here?" he asked.

I glared at him. "In all my spare time?"

He shrugged. "You wouldn't need to do it. Fairy painters could finish a job like this in less than an hour. You just need to choose the colors. That black banister is an eyesore. What was Gareth thinking?"

"Maybe after Mumford's trial," I said. "Then I'll have time to focus on frivolous things like paint colors."

"It isn't frivolous," he countered. "This is your home now. It should reflect who you are."

I looked around the room. "I wouldn't even know where to begin. The largest space I ever had to decorate was a fraction of the size of this."

"I'll help you."

My head jerked toward him. "You will?"

"Unless you don't want me to."

I squinted at him. "Why are you being so nice to me?" In truth, it was an unfair question. Daniel had been nothing but nice to me since my arrival.

"I need a reason?" he queried. "I think that says more about you than it does about me."

He was probably right.

"I'm sorry," I said. "I'm just stressed out."

He squeezed my shoulders and I tried to pretend I didn't feel anything when his fingers pressed into me. A crush on a fallen angel was a bad idea...wasn't it?

"You're under a fair amount of pressure," he said. "I'm actually quite impressed with how well you've handled yourself. A weaker human—I mean, witch—might have crumbled."

"There's still time," I said. And plenty of it, apparently.

Daniel turned in a circle, taking in the entire foyer. "How do you feel about beige? Too boring?"

"Actually, I think a light beige would really brighten up the space, especially once these blackout curtains come down."

Daniel walked over to the nearest window and, in one swift movement, removed the offending item. "There. How's that?"

Sunlight streamed in through the stained glass window. It was magnificent.

"Do the other ones," I said eagerly.

Daniel moved from window to window, stripping away the sun's obstacles. I regretted leaving the curtains for as long as I had. The room was already transformed and the walls weren't even painted yet.

"That's an improvement, wouldn't you say?" He

folded his bulging arms across his chest, looking satisfied.

"I would. Thank you."

Magpie trotted down the stairs, took one look at the windows, and hissed. He immediately turned around and went back upstairs.

I shrugged. "Can't please everybody."

Next he eyed the broken banister. "I heard about the murder weapon."

"I'm sure the whole town knows by now." What had it been since the discovery? Five hours?

"The elves here do amazing woodwork," he said. "I can help you get this fixed up whenever you're ready."

"Daniel, you don't have to help..."

He stopped and looked at me. "You think I'm going to let Demetrius do it? That guy has the taste of a doodlebug."

"A doodlebug? Is that a real thing?"

He cocked an eyebrow. "Of course. They're like ants. They drag their bottoms in the dirt and leave drawings behind."

Okay then.

"Have you heard any news from the sheriff's office?" I asked. "Any results from forensics?"

He shook his head. "Not yet. The sheriff has

really taken a dislike to you." He paused and grinned. "Which only makes most residents like you more."

"He's that popular, huh?"

"Sheriff Hugo has been sheriff for a long time," Daniel explained. "I think at some point we'll demand a regime change."

"Astrid seems capable." And scary.

"She's extremely capable, probably one of the reasons Sheriff Hugo is such a difficult toddler most of the time. He's afraid Astrid is going to swoop in and steal all his toys."

"Is that why he doesn't like me?" I asked. "He's afraid I'm going to steal his toys?"

"He's afraid you're going to make him look incompetent, which he is, and you rightfully have."

"If he's so incompetent, why keep him? The council seems to have their act together. Can't they appoint a replacement?"

Daniel fiddled with a loose cornice. "He and Mayor Knightsbridge are thick as thieves. Until she agrees to replace him, I'm afraid he's the head of law enforcement."

Too bad for Spellbound.

"Listen," he said. "I have time now. Why don't we fly over to the hardware store and choose paint for the rooms on the main floor?"

"Because I promised myself I wouldn't make this place mine until I'd earned it," I said.

"Emma, you're too tough on yourself, but if it makes you happy, we'll just choose the colors. We won't do anything with them until you're ready."

He really was sweet.

"I was also going to run through Mumford's case again before I made dinner."

He peered at me suspiciously. "What do you have to make for dinner?"

"I've been to the market," I said defensively.

He reached for my hand. "Come on. Take a break from all this crime and let me treat you to dinner, then we'll swing by the hardware store afterward."

I wondered how much of this attention was the result of Demetrius's interest in me. Would Daniel be here now if he hadn't seen me out with the vampire? The most gorgeous angel in the world just took my hand and asked me to dinner. Did I really care about his motivation?

"Any chance you brought a car?" I asked.

He tilted his head. "You'll be fine."

"I really won't. It isn't far. We can walk." If my feet could curse, they'd be reeling off a string of them right now.

"We can pick up a potion to ease your feet pain, too," Daniel said.

I glanced quizzically at him.

"You keep shifting your weight," he said. "I'm guessing your feet are bothering you."

"They are," I admitted.

"Then we'll buy you a potion before dinner," he said. "There's a place right near the town square."

"Okay, but I can't be out too late," I said. "Tomorrow is an important day."

"Don't worry. I'll be respectful of your needs."

That sounded promising.

"I just need to feed Magpie and then we can go."

"What about the owl?"

"Sedgwick hunts his own food." Thank goodness. I didn't love the idea of feeding him live mice. I wasn't a fan of mice, but it didn't mean I wanted to hand deliver them to death's door.

I hustled into the kitchen and refilled Magpie's water dish before restocking the food. Magpie appeared out of nowhere, rubbing against my leg.

"You smelled it from upstairs, didn't you?"

Magpie meowed.

"Do me a favor and be nice to Daniel," I said. "I want him to come here as often as he likes. If you're mean, he won't want to do that. Understand?"

The cat hissed at me.

"If you play ball, there's an extra can of tuna in it for you."

I waited for a revised response. Sure enough, Magpie gave me a sweet meow and swished his tail.

"I'm glad we understand each other," I said, and opened the can of tuna.

Dinner was at the nicest restaurant in town, a place called Serendipity right at the bottom of the town square. I was a little embarrassed by my casual clothes and lack of makeup, but no one seemed to mind. In fact, I noticed all variety of outfits among the guests. Everyone seemed to know Daniel. He was greeted with kisses from most of the females we met and a firm handshake from the males. If he'd slept with any of their daughters or ruined any of their marriages, no one said so. I guess it was the upscale ambience. It demanded good behavior.

"Next time warn me," I said, as we sat down at an intimate table at the back of the restaurant.

"About what?"

I looked pointedly at my outfit. "I came straight from the office. I didn't even comb my hair."

He grinned at me. "At least your socks match."

He had a point. There were plenty of monsters in Spellbound, but no sock monsters.

"I don't want to get a reputation as the slob," I said. And, honestly, I didn't want to look bad in front of Daniel. Not that I would admit that to him. Ever.

"I keep forgetting you don't know a lot of spells yet," he said. "The witches I dated were always able to switch things up with a snap of their fingers."

I peered across the menu at him. "Exactly how many witches have you dated?"

He appeared thoughtful. "Do you need an exact number? I can spitball it."

"You know what? Forget it. I don't think I want to know." I focused on the menu options. Every dish sounded divine.

"Choose anything you like," Daniel said. "I've never had a bad meal here."

"I want to be careful about what I pick," I told him. "I don't want to risk my stomach not settling. I'm already stressed about tomorrow."

He smiled at me over top of the menu. "You're going to be great. It sounds to me like you've been giving this case one hundred percent."

Daniel was so upbeat on my behalf. I really liked that quality about him. "Considering I don't know the first thing about criminal law, especially in Spellbound, I had to go through all the paperwork with a fine-tooth comb."

"If I ever get arrested for anything, I'd definitely want you as my public defender."

My heart skipped a beat. "Thanks, Daniel. That's so nice of you to say."

Just then, a couple passed by our table. I couldn't tell what kind of creatures they were because they looked human. The woman leaned down and said to me, "Next time you curse Sheriff Hugo, make sure it's permanent."

"But it was an accident," I said, but she was already out of earshot. I looked back at Daniel. "What was that about?"

"Summer Hansen. Her son Dirk was arrested a few months ago for trespassing. She hates Sheriff Hugo."

"Werewolves?" I asked.

"Werebears."

"That's a thing?" I said. I guess it was no stranger than a wereferret.

"There are a decent number of shifters in Spellbound. Gareth was on pretty good terms with the pack leaders. You should pay them a visit when you get a chance. Get to know them. They're a powerful group here and it will only make your job easier to make them feel important."

"Thanks for the tip. Are there are any groups that absolutely don't get along?"

"Usually it's more to do with a history between specific members of the groups."

"Like you and Mayor Knightsbridge's daughter? Or you and Meg?"

His brow lifted. "I'm not that guy anymore, Emma."

"Says you."

A floating notepad came over and we placed our orders. I guess it saved on hiring costs.

"Do you ever think that one day you'll wake up and the curse will be broken?"

"No," he said flatly.

"What would you do if that happened?" I asked. "Where would you go?"

"I don't allow myself to indulge in such fantasies," he said. "They only lead to heartbreak."

A life without dreams. What a depressing thought.

"What about you?" he asked. "What did you fantasize about back in...Where are you from?"

"Lemon Grove, Pennsylvania," I said, and took a sudden interest in the shiny cutlery. I had no problem asking questions, but it was hard for me to talk about personal issues. "I guess I dreamed about what all orphans dream about—being reunited with my parents. I carry them with me every day."

"Their loss?"

My brow furrowed. "No, Daniel. Their love."

CHAPTER 17

THE NEXT MORNING I felt refreshed and ready to tackle Mumford's case. As frustrating as he could be at times, Daniel had a way of making me feel like I could take on the world. Must be the angel in him.

I left my house with a spring in my step, and ran into Darcy and Calliope Minor as they pedaled their bicycles past the front of the house. Each set of handlebars came equipped with a wicker basket. I realized upon closer inspection that the wheels weren't actually turning. The bicycles were gliding through the air.

Calliope pressed her handbrakes when she saw me. "Hey, neighbor. Congratulations. I heard you found the murder weapon."

Darcy's eyes gleamed. "Serves that old centaur right for being such a condescending..."

"Darcy." Calliope's warning tone was abundantly clear.

"It's okay," I said. "He and I aren't exactly pals."

"We heard you were out with Daniel last night," Calliope said.

"And Demetrius Hunt before that," Darcy added. "You need to watch out for yourself. Those two will eat a sweet little witch like you alive."

"Not to mention you'll have half the females in Spellbound hating your guts," Calliope said. "Trust me, you do not want that. Some of them are lethal."

"They've both shown me nothing but kindness so far," I said. Mixed in with the occasional insult.

"Can I give you a lift into town?" Calliope asked. "I'm heading to the bookstore to help Juliet with new stock."

"I would love that," I said, "but there's only one seat."

Calliope pressed a button the side of the seat and it extended another foot. "Not anymore."

I climbed onto the back of the bike. "So these are part magic and part invention?"

"Yes. Quinty designed them. Have you met him?" Calliope asked.

"Not yet." Judging from the size of the town, I

imagined there were hundreds of residents I still hadn't met.

"Quinty's an elf," Darcy said. "He's a little unpopular with the other elves. They tend to be purists. They don't like to mix magic with their handiwork."

I shrugged. "Whatever works."

As much as I disliked heights, the bicycle remained close enough to the ground that I didn't feel too anxious.

We arrived at my office much faster than if I'd walked.

"Thank you so much," I said, scooting off the backseat. "I'll have to look into one of these. It's pretty handy."

Calliope rang the bell on her handlebar. "See you around, neighbor."

I went inside to greet Althea. She was on her knees, mopping up a puddle on the floor.

"Everything okay?" I asked.

"I knocked over your coffee," she said. "I'm so sorry. I'd even gotten an extra shot of confidence in it this morning because of your big day."

I grabbed another dish towel from the nearby counter and handed it to her. "You're so thoughtful."

"I'll go grab you another one as soon as I clean up this mess."

"Thanks, Althea. You're the best."

"Should I get one for Mumford, too?"

"It might be cold by the time he gets here."

She craned her neck to look at me. "He's already here."

Oh.

"In that case, I guess you should. No extra shot of anything for him." I needed him to be as authentic as possible today.

I swept into my office and, sure enough, Mumford was seated across from my desk, reading the newspaper.

"It's nice to know newspapers are alive and well here," I said.

"Are they not in the human world?" he asked, closing the paper.

"Not anymore."

He made a thoughtful noise at the back of his throat.

"How are you feeling?" I asked. "Ready to get this over with?"

He rubbed his hands together. "Very much so."

I dropped by handbag onto the desk and went over to inspect him. "Let me have a look at your neck. Your bandage has come loose again."

I lightly gripped the edge of the cotton pad.

"Leave it," he snapped, and jerked his head away. "It's fine."

"It isn't fine," I scolded him. "You can't have the bandage hanging off during the trial. It will be too distracting."

I resumed trying to adhere the bandage, but it fell to the floor.

"Oops, sorry." I was about to scoop it up when I noticed the swelling had reduced significantly. "You know what? I don't think you need the bandage after all. The ointment has worked wonders." I'd have to thank Boyd the next time I saw him.

"Good. Can we get back to business?" he asked, trying to move me back toward my desk. "Your propensity for distraction isn't one of your best qualities." Mumford seemed to find my invasion of his personal space offensive all of the sudden.

"You're grumpy for someone who's about to be acquitted," I told him.

I picked up the bandage off the floor and noticed something stuck to the cotton. I recognized it immediately. A splinter of wood, painted black. As nonchalantly as I could, I returned to my desk and opened the top of my handbag.

"I think you're going to do really well today." I continued to chatter, trying to keep him focused on my words rather than my actions. "Now if I can just find a working pen—silly me, I mean a quill, don't I? I'll never get used to Spellbound."

"You seem to be coping fine from what I can see," he said. "You've got all variety of handsome males interested in you. What's that like? To have the attention of someone you find desirable?"

I slipped the wand out of the handbag and quickly tucked it into my back pocket.

"Are you talking about Begonia?" I asked casually.

His chin jerked upward. "What do you know about Begonia?"

"I got the impression you liked her," I said. "That's all."

My act of casual interest apparently wasn't good enough. Mumford launched himself across the desk, snarling like a rabid animal. His horrible, disfigured hands clutched my throat and squeezed.

"Think you're clever, do you?" Spit flew from his enraged mouth and landed on my cheeks. If I weren't so frightened, I'd be totally grossed out.

"What...are...you...doing?" I choked out.

"You know I gave Begonia the emerald, don't you? Don't deny it."

I couldn't deny anything when I couldn't speak.

"And you found the splinter, didn't you?" he

demanded, continuing to throttle me. "I knew it was still in there. I could feel it, but I couldn't get the blasted thing out."

He was slowly crushing my airway. It took all of my focus to stay conscious and reach a hand to my back pocket. If I could no longer speak, how could I possibly do a spell? Then I remembered Lady Weatherby's lesson. *The witch's will is just as important as the wand and the incantation.* I had to try. There was no other choice.

I whipped out my wand and shoved it into his stomach. In my head, I shouted, *Red and black/major blowback.*

Mumford shot backward, straight over the desk, and slammed against the far wall. Pieces of drywall cracked around him. He slumped over and slid to the floor.

I stayed behind the desk, but continued to hold out my wand for good measure. I hoped he stayed unconscious. I didn't think I could do any spells more powerful than Blowback. I was lucky I managed that one.

The door to my office flew open and the sheriff galloped inside, followed by his deputy and Boyd, the druid healer. They saw me with my wand outstretched and shifted to the object of my wrath, noting Mumford on the floor beside them.

"Are you okay, Miss Hart?" Sheriff Hugo asked.

His deputy removed a pair of shining golden handcuffs from her belt. Enchanted, I assumed. Astrid slapped the cuffs onto Mumford just as he regained consciousness.

"Yes, I'm fine." My throat burned, but I was still alive and relatively unharmed.

Mumford glared at me from beneath hooded eyelids. "You'll regret this. Remember, you're trapped here now, just like the rest of us. When I get out, I will find you."

"What makes you think you'll ever get out?" Astrid asked. "Murder *and* theft? You'll be lucky to escape the death penalty."

"He'll need a new lawyer," I said. "I think I'm officially disqualified."

The sheriff snarled at Mumford. "I don't know that a lawyer is necessary anymore."

So things worked a little differently in Spellbound. Not much of a surprise really.

Boyd crossed the room to examine my neck. "You're bruised."

Gently, I touched the sore spots. "He tried to choke me."

"Allow me." Boyd rubbed his hands together and placed his fingertips on my neck. He closed his eyes and hummed until the pain began to dissipate.

"How did you do that?" I asked.

"Ancient druids have our own special brand of magic," he said. "You'll learn, once you've been here longer."

"Thank you," I said, stretching my neck from side to side. "What made you come here anyway?"

"I received the rest of the test results from Mumford's office visit. The test showed traces of pizzazz, found in certain brands of fairy paint. It made me suspicious so I called Sheriff Hugo."

"I found the splinter in his neck when I went to fix the bandage," I said. "I went to retrieve my wand, but he saw me. I only pieced it together at the last second. Seeing the splinter was the nail in the coffin for Gareth's murder." I winced at my choice of analogy.

Mumford laughed bitterly. "I'll never tell you where I've hidden the rest of the jewels."

"You may change your mind after spending a few minutes alone with Astrid," Sheriff Hugo said with a smile. "She can be a tough interrogator."

Mumford paled at the sight of Astrid cracking her knuckles.

"I've been meaning to practice my methods of persuasion," Astrid said. "Now I have the perfect opportunity."

"Will you tell Begonia that I did mean for her to have the ring?" Mumford asked me.

"She won't care," I said. "Not when she hears that you killed Gareth. Begonia liked Gareth." It seemed that everyone did.

Sheriff Hugo looked at me. "So the splinter was from the missing support post in Gareth's house, wasn't it?"

"Yes," I said. "Gareth must have figured out that Mumford really had stolen the jewels and confronted him in the foyer of his house. He never expected Mumford to pull a stake on him. They struggled and Gareth must've managed to skim Mumford's neck with the support post."

"So where's the weapon, Miss Clever Wand?" Mumford asked. "No weapon means no physical evidence."

"The splinter is the physical evidence," I said. "We already know you burned the murder weapon in Gareth's fireplace, and then took the body to the woods so no one would suspect Gareth was killed at home."

"Only he didn't realize at first that a piece of

evidence was lodged in his neck," Boyd said. "No wonder he got an infection."

"I tried to dig out the splinter on my own," Mumford admitted. "But I couldn't get it."

"And you made the wound worse in the process," Boyd said, and shook his head. "Did you even bother to wash your hands before you rooted around in there?"

I wrinkled my nose in disgust.

Astrid forced Mumford to his feet. "I look forward to our conversation," she said. Mumford looked far less happy about it.

"I'll be sure to tell Lady Weatherby about your successful spell casting," Boyd said. "You know, put in a good word for you."

I needed a good word put in for me if I wanted to be allowed back into the academy. "Thanks. I appreciate it."

Boyd smiled. "Don't mention it."

CHAPTER 18

I WAS RECOVERING at home in bed when Sedgwick alerted me to visitors.

Are you decent? he asked.

"You're not blind," I replied.

But you're wearing those fuzzy clothes, he said. *I have no sense of their propriety.*

"They're pajamas. It's fine," I said, and then added quickly, "unless it's Demetrius or Daniel."

Despite the warning, the knock on the bedroom door startled me. I was relieved when Laurel's head poked through the crack.

"Emma? Can we come in?"

"Of course." I sat up and smoothed my hair.

"We heard about what happened with Mumford," Sophie said. "Are you okay?"

"Never better," I said. "Tiffany didn't let me down."

"Tiffany?" Laurel queried.

"That's what I've named my wand," I said.

They exchanged glances.

"What?" I said. "I named my car, too. I name things. That's what I do."

Begonia made herself comfortable on the edge of my bed. "When did you realize that Mumford was the killer?"

"I think my subconscious was already trying to tell me, but I wasn't listening. When I saw the splinter, something clicked into place."

Laurel plopped beside me on the other side of the bed. "So the goblin was the killer and the thief. Two crimes. One criminal."

"Gareth had figured out Mumford was the thief," I said. "That's why Mumford killed him. He committed one crime to hide another. Because of the hefty sentence for theft, he probably felt it was the worth the risk to silence Gareth."

"Bummer," Begonia said. "And to think I defended Mumford when people bullied him."

"You were one of the reasons I put it together, actually," I said. "I remembered that he'd mentioned you in one of our first meetings. And then you received one of Deacon's emeralds from the burglary."

"Good thing I'd already given it to you," Begonia said. "I certainly wouldn't want anything to do with it now."

"So what's next?" Millie asked. "Are you going to stay in bed all day?"

Laurel tugged on my arm. "Get dressed."

"And come with us if you want to live," Begonia said, in a terrible attempt at an Austrian accent.

I stared at her. "Did you seriously just reference *The Terminator*?"

She merely gave me a coy look and shrugged. How could she possibly know lines from a 1980's movie?

"Come on, Emma," Sophie urged. "We have somewhere to show you that's far more interesting than your bedroom wall. You don't want to miss this."

Thirty minutes later, I was barreling across town in Millie's blue jalopy. I'd begged them not to take me on a broom because I'd had enough near death experiences in the past twenty-four hours.

We continued out of town and eventually parked near a remote hillside. "Where are we?"

"You'll see," Millie said cryptically.

I followed the girls to the side of the hill. Sophie placed a palm on the dirt and muttered an incantation. A door appeared and she smiled at me over her shoulder.

"Welcome," she said, and we went inside.

"You have an underground lair?" I asked in disbelief, surveying the room in wonder and admiration.

To say the room was cavernous was an understatement. The walls were lined with books and there were plenty of seating areas, including beanbag chairs, couches, and recliners. A huge gilded mirror hung on the feature wall.

"Technically it belongs to the coven," Millie said. "But it's a designated place for younger witches to get away from the older generations. We are the only four who know the magic words to unlock the door."

"And now we're going to share it with you," Begonia added, and slung an arm along my shoulders.

A large basket in the corner of the room caught my eye. "Do you still play with dolls?"

Four guilty faces looked back at me.

"Not exactly," Sophie said. "Laurel, why don't you show her?"

Laurel reached into the basket and produced a puppet of…

I gasped. "It's Lady Weatherby." The likeness was astounding.

The other witches laughed as I rushed over to examine the contents of the basket. There was a puppet for every major witch in the coven. I placed Weatherby's puppet on my hand.

"Now Miss Hart," I said, imitating Lady Weatherby's clipped tone. "Stop embarrassing this coven with your amateur performance."

"Sometimes we use them as voodoo dolls," Begonia admitted.

"You stab them with pins?" I asked.

"No," Sophie said. "We cast little spells on them. Small curses that they wouldn't necessarily attribute to us."

"Like a new wart on the nose," Laurel said proudly.

I laughed. "So these weren't passed down from other witches?"

"No," Millie said. "We made these ourselves. The older witches think we're not very powerful, but we're far more capable than they realize. And we prove it all the time. They just don't know it."

"Wow," I breathed. "Remind me not to get on

your bad sides. If I see a puppet of me in here, I know I'm in trouble."

"We don't torture them every day," Begonia said. "Only if they are being particularly annoying."

"Or like the time Ginger muscled her way in on your date with Ivan, the werewolf," Sophie said to Millie.

Millie plucked out the red-haired puppet and showed it to me. "I put itching powder on the puppet's head. Ginger scratched her head all night. Ivan thought she had fleas and kept his distance."

"Thank you so much for sharing this with me," I said. For the first time, I felt like they trusted me. That I was truly one of them.

"Oh, but there's more," Begonia said, and gestured to the oversized mirror.

"That is pretty," I admitted. "But not as cool as torture puppets."

Begonia closed her eyes and performed a low chant. Then she pointed her wand at the mirror and it began to glow.

"Is it a teleportation device?" I asked.

"Of a sort," Sophie replied.

I continued to watch as the beveled glass turned black and then an image appeared. An image I recognized.

"Arnold Schwarzenegger?" I couldn't believe my eyes. The mirror was some kind of magic television.

"We watch all sorts of movies and television from the human world," Millie said. "But we keep it quiet. We know the coven wouldn't like it."

"Why not?" I asked.

"Because they're not fans of the human influence," Sophie said. "You guys have kinda ruined nature and our powers are steeped in nature."

"Hey," I said. "I'm one of you, remember?" And I always recycled.

"If you tell us what you want to watch, we can find it," Laurel said. "The spell is simple."

My head was spinning with ideas. "You really are more capable than they give you credit for."

Sophie twirled a Meg puppet above her head. "Just because I can't do the Blowback spell without a hitch doesn't mean I can't do anything right. They don't seem to get the fact that some of our talents lie in other areas of witchcraft."

It would probably be the same for me. After all, I wasn't even descended from the same coven. We already knew my familiar was an owl, not a cat. Who knew what else we'd discover about my abilities?

"Who wants popcorn?" Begonia asked. She

pointed her wand at the coffee table and an overflowing bucket of popcorn appeared.

"This is definitely going to be my favorite place," I said, and popped a kernel into my mouth. It was salty and buttery, just the way I liked it.

"Are there any movies you recommend that we might not have seen?" Sophie asked.

My lips curved as an idea came to mind. "Have you watched any human movies about witches?"

They shook their heads.

"Just *The Wizard of Oz*," Laurel said.

"That's a classic," I told her. "But I've got a whole slew of movies I think you'll enjoy." I looked at Begonia. "Conjure up a movie called *The Craft*."

CHAPTER 19

Now that I'd made good on my promise to finish Mumford's case and find Gareth's murderer, I felt ready to start going through Gareth's disco vampire cave in the basement.

As I unhooked the disco ball from the ceiling, I caught sight of someone in a black suit. I whipped out my wand, ready to use the Shield spell. Unfortunately for me, I misjudged the distance between the wand and the disco ball. The wand smacked hard against the shiny ball and went flying from my fingertips. It clattered onto the floor.

"You are a wee bit clumsy, aren't you?" a voice asked.

The figure came into focus and I realized with a start that he was not entirely solid. "Who are you and what are you doing in my house?"

He chuckled politely. "I think you'll find this is technically my house." He sighed and looked around the room. "Or was."

I squinted. "Gareth?"

He spread his arms wide. "In the flesh." His brow wrinkled. "Or not." He made an exaggerated effort to touch my arm, but his hand kept gliding through me.

Fabulous. After all I'd been through, now I had a vampire ghost to contend with. "Where have you been?" I demanded. "You could have saved me a whole lot of trouble if you'd shown up sooner."

"Processing my death took ages," he said, with an exaggerated roll of his eyes. "You wouldn't believe the bureaucracy."

"Trust me. I'm from the human world. I believe it." I inclined my head. "So why are you back? Your murder has been solved. Shouldn't you be going into the light or something?" Or maybe somewhere less pleasant, given that he was damned. I had no clue. I just knew that I wasn't in the market for a dead, or undead, roommate.

"Excellent work with figuring it out, by the way," Gareth said. "I do appreciate your efforts on my behalf."

"No problem." I placed a hand on my hip. "So why are you here?"

His shoulders sagged. "They wouldn't let me through because I was from Spellbound. They said the true death was not enough to break the curse."

I'd need to pass that tidbit along to Daniel, save him the trouble of suicide. "Then shouldn't there be ghosts all over town?"

"There probably are," he said. "But only certain witches can see ghosts. Everybody knows that."

Well, if I wasn't sure whether I was a witch before, I was certainly convinced now.

"So the coven can see ghosts?" No one had mentioned that before.

"No, I don't believe so. It must be a special trait of the coven you're descended from."

Was there a way to genetically mutate myself? I wasn't interested in communicating with ghosts on a regular basis. Or any basis.

"Why couldn't I see ghosts before?" It was one thing to discover I was a witch, but I would think I'd know if I had some kind of spiritual awareness. In the human world, I was one of the least spiritual people I knew. I couldn't even do yoga without giggling.

"I suspect you triggered your witchy powers once you crossed the border into Spellbound," he replied.

"My witchy powers don't seem very potent," I said. "Unless it involves torturing Lady Weatherby."

A faint smile played upon his lips. "You're wreaking havoc over at the ASS Academy?"

"In small doses," I admitted.

He laughed. "Excellent. I shall look forward to your daily reports." He frowned. "Speaking of doses, I notice you have a bit of trouble in the sleep department."

"My life story," I said. "My grandparents said I was a difficult sleeper from the time I was born. They blamed my mother. Apparently she held me to get me to sleep instead of putting me down in the crib." The idea of being held by my mother was so appealing, I nearly burst into tears at the thought.

"Hasn't anyone recommended a sleep potion?" Gareth asked. "You have a coven of witches at your disposal. Use them."

"I haven't told anyone about my sleep issues." I didn't want to come across as a whiner, not while I was still getting to know everyone.

"Then you need to start opening up to your witch friends," he said. "No one can help you if they don't know there's a problem."

Great. My roommate intended to double as my

armchair therapist. Just what I needed to ease my anxiety.

"Can't you go hang out at the country club or something?" I asked. "It will feel weird to have you haunting my house. I don't even know you."

That wasn't strictly true. Throughout my investigation into his murder, I got a sense of the kind of person—vampire—Gareth was. I liked him. I just never expected to be sharing close quarters with him.

"It seems I can move freely about the town," he said. "But this is my home base, just as it is yours."

"Can you manipulate objects at all?" I queried. I was already imagining the fun we could have on the golf course at the expense of his vampire buddies.

"I'm not certain," he said. "They don't exactly give you a rule book on the way out."

"Sounds like there was plenty of red tape. Maybe a rule book wouldn't be such a burden to add."

"Oh, there's my Magpie," he exclaimed.

The cat came running over to him, meowing and purring. Gareth kneeled down to greet him.

"He can see you?" I asked. It was a touching reunion, despite the lack of…touching.

"All cats are part witch," he said. "Everybody knows that." He looked up at me and I noticed tears glistening in his eyes. "Thank you for taking care of him. Most people wouldn't have been willing to take on a cat like Magpie. I'm fully aware he isn't the most sociable creature."

Or the most attractive. "He's not too excited about Sedgwick moving in," I admitted.

Gareth blinked. "Who's Sedgwick?"

"My owl," I said. "All witches here have owls. Everybody knows that." I smiled.

"I always sent my letter by elf," he said. "Elf Express is a very reliable company."

"I'll make a note of it."

"So what do you intend to do with my disco ball?" he asked.

"One of your friends asked for it."

"Samson?"

"How did you know?"

He punched a fist into his palm. "I knew he had his eye on it. 'Oh no,' he would say, 'it's as tacky as a succubus in church.'"

I set the disco ball onto the floor and moved on to the closet.

"Great balls of fire, Gareth," I said. "You were a clothes hoarder." The further I worked my way into the back of his closet, the more clothes I found. I pulled out a pair of black leather trousers. "When did you ever wear these?"

He shrugged. "I went through a club phase."

"Are there even clubs here?" I asked.

"Of course. There's a good one over by Shamrock Casino. You should go sometime. Loosen up those knotty muscles of yours. You walk like a tin soldier."

I glanced at him over my shoulder. "I'm loose."

"Like a broomstick."

"Hey," I objected. "Cut me some slack. New girl in town, remember?" I continued to rummage through sweaters and tweed jackets. Lots of tweed. I yanked a hanger from the closet. "Was this from your academic phase?"

Gareth grimaced. "Burn that one. It's hideous."

A flash of pink on the shelf caught my eye. "Hang on." I reached up and removed the item from the closet. "Isn't this Alison's pink cardigan?"

At least he had the decency to look sheepish.

"She's been looking for this."

"I figured. She used to wear it all the time. I knew it was a risk to take it."

I held the cardigan against me. It was pretty, with shiny sequins along the trim. "Does it smell like her? Is that why you kept it?" I understood all about affection for familiar scents.

He wrinkled his nose. "What kind of oddball do you take me for?"

I blinked. "Did you just want a keepsake? Something to remember your time together?" If not for sentimental reasons, then why bother?

He heaved a dramatic sigh and stared longingly at the cardigan. "I took it because I like sparkly things and it fit me perfectly. Are you happy now? You've discovered my secret."

I glanced from Gareth back to the cardigan in my hand. "You were a cross-dresser?"

"Not really, just the occasional item." He paused. "But I am gay." He splayed his hands. "There I said it. After all these centuries, I've finally come out of the coffin."

I gave him my best slow clap. "Yes, very brave of you, waiting until your true death."

"I beg your pardon," he said. "This is a momentous event."

I continued rifling through the closet, creating piles for donation. "I'll take your word for it."

"This is outrageous," he said. "I've never told anyone my secret. Not Alison. Not the other vampires. Not even Magpie."

"Oh, I'm sure Magpie knew." Cats knew everything. I was pretty sure that, deep down, Alison knew, too. That was probably at the heart of why they fought all the time. They loved each other, but not in the way they needed to in order to continue as a couple.

Gareth began to glide around the room, the ghostly version of pacing. "I should have come out to someone else. You're clearly the wrong person."

I held up a colorfully striped shirt. "Do you want me to throw you a gay pride parade? Because we definitely have the necessary outfits."

"You're impossible," he huffed.

"Everything about my life is impossible, and yet here we are." I tossed the garish shirt into the 'donate' pile, walked away from my gay dead/undead roommate, and headed upstairs to the kitchen to make a tuna sandwich.

CHAPTER 20

After a long day of sorting and organizing, I was ready to stop for the day. I'd only paused briefly to feed Magpie and argue with Gareth over whether beige was the right color for the foyer. He was pushing for canary yellow.

"You seem to be under the mistaken impression that you get a vote," I said. "One corporeal being equals one vote."

"You said you want it brighter in here," he argued.

"Brighter, not blinding," I replied.

Incoming, Sedgwick said, swooping into the living room. I was in the process of finding a better home for my blue and yellow pot and decided to try the huge mantel.

Are you announcing yourself or someone else? I asked.

Daniel appeared in the doorway. "That's a good place for it."

I stepped back to admire the pot. "It is, isn't it? Thanks."

"I wanted to come by and see how you're feeling," he said. "I heard you took Mumford out with one spell."

I nodded. "And Lady Weatherby has invited me back to school, starting tomorrow."

"That's great news." He advanced toward me. "I hope that..."

I held up a hand. "Be careful what you say," I warned him. "I have a new roommate."

Gareth appeared behind Daniel, his arms folded. "I think you'll find I'm a very old roommate."

"Whatever," I said.

Daniel's brow furrowed. "Who are you talking to?"

"Gareth. He's the roommate."

Daniel's blue eyes widened. "Gareth is here?" He looked to the left and right of me, but, of course, saw nothing.

"Technically, his ghost is here," I said.

"Tell him I've always loved his style," Gareth said.

"I'll tell him no such thing," I said hotly.

Daniel squinted. "What does he want you to tell me?"

"That he looks scorching in those tight pants," Gareth said, eyeing Daniel's muscled body appreciatively. I knew exactly what he was doing because I'd already done it.

A hand flew to my hip. "Hundreds of years in the coffin and now you're going hell for leather?"

"What are you talking about?" Daniel queried.

"Never mind." I looked at Gareth. "Can we please have privacy? If we're going to live together, you need to respect my boundaries."

Gareth huffed. "Fine. I'll go see what Magpie is up to."

"Probably licking his balls," I said. "Between that and stalking my owl, he doesn't seem to do much else."

"Is he gone?" Daniel asked.

"Yes. Sorry about that. It's going to take some getting used to." Like everything else in Spellbound.

"Did you always have the ability to see ghosts?" he asked.

"No. Thankfully, I was a ghost virgin until Gareth." I already suffered from anxiety. Seeing ghosts my whole life probably would have tipped me over into catatonic territory.

"Too bad he didn't show up in time to name his murderer," Daniel said. "Could have saved you from a tussle with a goblin."

I pretended to crack my knuckles. "Goblin takedown. Just another day for a newbie witch."

"Are you busy?" he asked.

"Nope. I am officially off duty."

"Perfect. I'd like you to come with me," he said, and held out his hand.

I stared at his open palm and my insides quivered. "Wherever we're going, can we get there on four wheels?" I'd even settle for two. The thought of flying made me queasy.

He gave me a rueful smile. "Afraid not. These are your best bet." He extended his white wings and gently flapped them. "You're a witch, remember? Sooner or later, you'll need to get comfortable in the air."

I doubted it was either possible or necessary, but now wasn't the time to argue.

"I really need to find the magic potion equivalent of Xanax," I said. Add it to my ever-growing list.

My hand slipped into his and we left the house together. "Maybe I should think about adding a widow's walk like the harpies have."

He grimaced. "We're having a perfectly nice

moment. Please don't ruin it with mention of the harpies." He stopped walking. "Are you ready?"

"There's really no dignified way of doing this," I said, and looped my arms around his neck. He lifted me off the ground and vaulted into the air. His wings caught the wind and we flew skyward until we cleared the rooftops.

"Dignity is overrated," he said. "You should try to open your eyes. You're missing the beautiful scenery."

I pried open one eye and glanced below. He was right. It was truly a picture postcard town. I saw the clock tower as we passed overhead, as well as the church steeple. We continued on, and I realized we were headed toward the place we'd met. Swan Lake.

The hills rose higher and so did we, until finally we reached the highest peak. It was the clifftop where I'd first seen him, ready to jump.

His wings flapped more slowly and he sailed down to the precipice, setting me gently on my feet.

"This is a little high for me," I said, edging backward. I didn't dare look at the water below. My heart was pounding and my palms were sweaty.

"Bear with me a moment," he said. "Don't worry. If you fall, you already know I can catch you."

I took a careful step forward. "Why did you want to bring me here?"

"For one thing, we're about to witness a gorgeous sunset."

I gazed at the streaks of orange, red, and gold racing across the sky. It was simply stunning.

"And for another thing?"

"To thank you," he said. "You were right about me." His expression clouded over. "I *was* suicidal that day. If I'm being honest, I've been suicidal for years."

"Why would you jump?" I asked. "Like you said, you have wings. You could have flown at any point before hitting the water."

"It's like cutting your wrists the wrong way," he said. "It was more of a cry for help." He stared down at the lake. "I was so tired of looking at this single body of water. Tired of the town square and the same bookstore and the same damn residents, day in and day out."

"Are you allowed to say 'damn'?"

He arched a blond eyebrow. "Kinda missing the point."

"I'm sorry," I said. I knew it couldn't be easy. Not for any of them.

"But then you came," he said. "And you were different. And you looked at the town and you were amazed. Your entire world was turned upside down, but did you crawl into a hole and hide? Did you wallow in self-pity?"

Maybe a little bit.

"Did you act like a fool and sleep with everything that moved?"

I held up a finger. "Um, no. That's not really my style..."

He gripped me by the shoulders. "You've lost everything and yet you still found the strength within yourself to get on with your life. And even more, to help others."

My face reddened. I wasn't accustomed to compliments, certainly not from someone like Daniel.

I wasn't sure what he wanted me to say. "Thank you?"

He pointed me toward the lake. "The last time I came here, this water looked dark and deep. Like a final resting place. I was ready to bring Alison and let her sing me to a watery grave. Now do you know what I see?"

"A place to kayak?"

"I see beauty. I see nature at its best. I see the potential for goodness where none existed before."

I peered into the shimmering water. "I see fish."

He grabbed my hand and pulled me toward him with enthusiasm. "I'm turning over a new leaf, Emma. All thanks to you. I'm going to start being present in the community, instead of resenting everyone. I'm going to redeem myself for my previous, hurtful behavior. From here on in, I'm swearing off the opposite sex."

"So you're only going to date men?"

"What?" He blinked. "No. I'm going to devote myself to the greater good. Even if that means volunteering for Darcy's annoying projects."

Fabulous. The hottest guy in town and I managed to turn him into a monk. The females in town would lynch me.

"Are you sure, Daniel?" I asked. "This seems like a major epiphany. Maybe it's just a phase. I mean, you can still contribute to the community without being celibate."

Please don't be celibate or I might throw myself off this cliff.

He leaned forward and, for one miraculous moment, I thought he was going to kiss me. My wish was about to come true! I closed my eyes and felt his lips brush…against my forehead.

Oh.

He rubbed his hands together excitedly. "Sunset's over. Are you ready to go home?"

I nodded, unable to bring myself to speak. I didn't want my emotions to betray me. Not now when he seemed so full of joy and possibility. How could I ruin it for him? Anyway, we'd only recently met. I was sure my feelings for him were fleeting. After all, he was the first angel I'd ever met. The novelty was sure to wear off and I'd start to be annoyed by his flaws. He probably picked his teeth with his fingernails. That was sufficiently unattractive. Yes, let's go with that.

I clasped my fingers around his neck and held on tightly. I tried to ignore the feel of his strong arms around me. I didn't need Daniel to be my boyfriend, right? It would be enough to have him as a friend, to help guide me through this new chapter in my life.

As we flew back over Spellbound toward the house, I began to relax and enjoy the ride. This was what Sedgwick did every day—flew back and forth across town. If he could do it, then so could I. Sedgwick was an unexpected surprise. To be fair, everything about this town was an unexpected surprise. I thought of all the wonderful and interesting inhabitants I'd met and looked forward to meeting those I hadn't. By the time Daniel lowered me to the front porch, I felt a renewed sense of hope.

"I'll see you tomorrow," Daniel said. "I'll bring you coffee at the office at nine."

"Make it nine-thirty," I said. "I'm sleeping in tomorrow."

I flung open the door and went inside. "Gareth," I called. "I'm home."

* * *

Thank you for reading **Curse the Day**! If you enjoyed it, please help other readers find this book ~

1. Write a review and post it on Amazon.

2. Sign up for my new releases via e-mail here http://eepurl.com/ctYNzf or like me on Facebook so you can find out about the next book before it's even available.

3. Look out for the next books in the series:

Doom and Broom, Book 2

Spell's Bells, Book 3

Lucky Charm, Book 4

Better Than Hex, Book 5